CRISPIN

THE END OF TIME

CRISPIN

THE END OF TIME

AVI

BALZER + BRAY

An Imprint of HarperCollins*Publishers*

Balzer + Bray is an imprint of HarperCollins Publishers.

Crispin: The End of Time

Copyright © 2010 by Avi

All rights reserved. Printed in the United States of America.

www.harpercollinschildrens.com

Library of Congress Cataloging-in-Publication Data is available.

ISBN 978-0-06-174080-0 (trade bdg.)

ISBN 978-0-06-174082-4 (lib. bdg.)

10 11 12 13 14 LP/RRDH 10 9 8 7 6 5 4 3 2 1

❖

First Edition

For Jo Ellen Priest Misakian

CRISPIN

THE END OF TIME

FRANCE, 1377 AD

"If you can go no farther than where you are,
God has shown you your destiny."
—attributed to St. Cyril

1

BEAR WAS DEAD.

That sweet and kindly man, the wisest I had ever known, the one I considered friend, teacher, and even father, was gone. Would that I could be half so fine. God keep his saintly soul!

Though I no longer had a father or a mother, I had, thanks be to God and Bear, a name: Crispin. And since I was bound to no land, kin, lord, or, for that matter, any man, I considered myself free. As long as I could keep myself out of bondage, I'd be true to Bear's teaching. And so it was that beyond all else, I was determined to keep my freedom.

I had but one friend. Her name was Troth. She had sailed to France with Bear and me from England. It was during that violent voyage and its aftermath that we met with such misfortune and Bear's awful death.

With his going, I was Troth's sole companion as she was mine. Our ages were much the same—far too young to be alone. But there was more than that: since Troth's twisted face brought rejection and fear, and garbled her speech—which I could best understand—I held myself as her shield. Was that not what Bear had done for me? I would do no less for her.

Bear had told us about Iceland. He proclaimed it a land without kings, lords, or armies. Men—he said—lived free there. If we went, we too could be free.

Though Bear's death burdened Troth and me with grief like stones upon our backs, we decided to go to that Iceland. God knows it was folly to seek a place when we did not know where it might be, other than "far north," as Bear had once said. But we took courage from a notion he had taught us: God offers many paths from which we may choose. If we put faith in ourselves, He would travel with us to the ends of the earth—and beyond.

And so we headed north, walking countless miles along narrow paths, through dense forests and by fallow fields. We passed through deserted lands, places ravaged by disease, poverty, and the endless wars between the French and

English. Ruins, graves, and desolation lay everywhere. It was as if God Himself had fled.

For the most part, we tried to keep to woodlands, avoiding roads and villages. Our greatest fear was that, being young and without protection, we would be forced into some kind of servitude. But in the wild woods wherein we wandered, we were in equal dread of thieves and brigands, the brutal outlaws who preyed on hapless travelers. All of which is to say we never felt completely safe.

From time to time, we did meet people: sore-footed pilgrims; peasants with their dirty, bleating sheep; chapmen selling ribbons and simple shards of saintly relics; and now and again an impoverished knight with his small troop of rusty-helmeted soldiers. They spoke languages unknown to us.

I tried asking about Iceland in hopes that someone might speak English, or at least recognize the name of the place and tell us how we could get there. The only response we received was empty stares. Looking beggarly—which, by Saint Francis, is how we must have appeared—we were for the most part ignored.

Though not big—nothing like Bear—I was taller than Troth. We were both thin, our bruised bodies filthy, our feet bare, our clothing mostly tattered. Troth, with her dark and staring eyes and her broken face, which she tried to hide with her long hair, often drew uneasy looks.

For food, we depended upon her knowledge of wild plants, the names of which I did not know—things taught to her by Old Aude, the midwife-healer who had raised her. Once I caught a scrawny rabbit, twice, pigeons, which fed us for a winking while. So it was we ate little, though flies and fleas feasted on us.

With every passing day, our hunger and weariness increased. The farther we went, the less we knew where we were. It was growing colder, too, with more leaves underfoot than on trees. In all of this, Troth did not utter a complaint, but I grew ever more aware of her growing exhaustion.

Then one night, after a daylong trudge, Troth threw herself down and cried, "I wish I'd never left England!"

I hardly knew what to say. "We can find our way" was my dull reply.

She sighed. "Crispin," she said gently, "we don't even know where we are."

"But we know where we're going," I insisted. "Once we reach Iceland, we'll be safe. We'll live free. It's such a peaceful land, there's bound to be plenty of food."

At first she said nothing. Then, in a voice seeped in sadness, she said, "It was peaceful with Aude."

"Troth, she was killed. We had to flee."

"But before, my days were calm," she went on, as if she were talking to herself. "We helped others when we could."

"Aude's wanting to help caused her death."

Troth glared at me reproachfully. "Wouldn't you care for the sick? We helped Bear when he was sick."

"God's truth," I admitted.

She closed her eyes. "Once Aude told me that the biggest worlds can best be found in the smallest places. Crispin, I don't need this . . . huge world."

Though I so wanted to care for her, I barely knew how to care for myself. "What would you have us do?" I said in exasperation.

"We need to learn how far Iceland is. Maybe . . . maybe it's too far."

I tried to push aside my own qualms by saying, "When we get there, it'll be worth everything."

She shook her head. "I don't know what your 'everything' is."

"Troth!" I cried. "What else are we to do? We're lost! We can't speak the language! The only thing Bear left us was his words. His . . . his promise. His pointing north." I held out empty hands. "That's all we have!"

Troth said nothing for a long time. Then, in a small, plaintive voice, she said, "We have to find out where we are."

"We can try," I agreed, exhausted.

"Anything is better than what we've been doing."

The next day we started to search for someplace to rest and eat, where we might discover the way to go. Four days later we came upon a small village, the first we'd seen in many days.

It was there our lives completely changed.

2

T WAS LATE AFTERNOON when we reached the village. There wasn't much to see. A narrow lane made its crooked way through a cluster of small timbered houses, all in poor repair. A few oxen, ragged sheep, and some scrawny chicks wandered free. Thin smoke rose from chimneys. Here and there were cabbage crofts, and farther out were narrow fields filled with stubbled grain. I saw a broken plow, a wagon with three wheels, and an old and crowded cemetery before which stood a small stone church. The whole village was tainted with the smells of rot and poverty.

The only unusual thing was that on a hill overlooking the village stood a large stone building with red roof tiles. At one end was a bell tower with a cross. I assumed it was another, bigger church. There seemed to be other buildings behind it, but I couldn't see them well. It did not matter: our interest lay in the village.

There were people about, mostly older men and women, plus some children. Their drab garb and weathered faces told me they were peasants. Offering no sign of welcome, they stared suspiciously at us from their doors.

If I had been with Bear, we would have entered the town with me playing the recorder and him dancing and juggling. By bringing rare merriment to such meager places, we always managed to earn a little bread. Alas, Troth and I had long ago lost our instruments. As for dancing, we had neither strength nor spirit. We needed to beg.

At length I spied an old man sitting on a bench before an open door. As I approached, he stared at me with red, runny eyes but made no movement nor offered any greeting.

"God be with you, master!" I called, making a clumsy bow.

He gazed at me.

"In the name of Jesus," I said louder, "our hunger

makes us beg for bread."

He continued to study me in silence. Then, pulling at his ruddy, grizzled chin with a bent hand, he barked, "*Parlez français!*"

Of course: he spoke French, and I only had my English. Stymied, all I could do was put forth cupped hands in a begging gesture. "Food," I said, and touched hand to mouth. "Food."

"Food," he echoed, without seeming to comprehend.

Other villagers began to edge near—if none too close—and considered us with uninviting looks. A few were holding staffs. One man clutched a rusty sword.

Alarmed, Troth drew near me as I tried to show our peaceful intent by more bowing, touching my belly, and holding out my hands. "Food!" I kept repeating to now one and then another.

A ragged boy—shoved by an elder—came forward. He halted at what he must have considered a safe distance. Even at that, he looked at us with disdain, wrinkling his nose as if disgusted. Someone shouted at him. With a hand gesture, the boy beckoned to us and headed away. Not knowing what else to do, we followed. The other people remained behind, but kept watching us.

The boy led us up the hill to that large church we had

first seen. As we drew nearer, the building seemed to grow in size, far bigger than I had realized. I saw no ornamentation. Windows were few. The stone walls were covered by entangled green vines, out of which bats flew.

The boy took us to an entryway, a massive pair of tall, wide doors built of bolt-studded wooden planks that were rounded at the top. On one of the doors, a large and rusty iron face of some fearful beast was attached. From its gaping, toothy jaws hung a knocking ring.

The boy stood on his toes, grabbed the ring, and thumped the door three times. Next moment he turned suddenly and spat at Troth's face. *"Laide!"* he cried, and bolted down the hill. I spun and started to give chase only to have Troth grab my sleeve and hold me back.

"Let him go," she said wearily, and wiped the spittle from her face.

I put my arm around her trembling shoulders. She said no more.

Not knowing what else to do—shivering from cold and distress—we waited by the door. By then the moon was just above the trees. Quite huge, its brightness turned the evening clouds blue. Overhead, bats flitted about in rapid, erratic flight. From a distance I heard the hooting of an owl. I kept glancing down the hill, fearful that other villagers would come and accost us.

A bell rang out loudly, enough to make me start. Shortly after, I heard the grinding sound of a turning lock. One of the double doors opened a crack.

Peering out of darkness was a woman's face—nothing but her face. Startled, it took me a moment to realize it was a nun in her long black habit, her pale face encased in a wimple. The burning candle she held in her hand revealed that she was tall, her face bore many lines, and her eyes seemed hard. Her mouth suggested firmness.

She lifted her candle, the better to look down at us. Under her gaze, Troth—as usual—shifted her hair to hide her face.

"God be with you, Sister," I muttered, not knowing what else to say.

The nun's eyes widened slightly. It was a few moments before she said, "Are you . . . English?" The words were spoken haltingly, with some puzzlement.

Elated she spoke our language, I made another bow. "We are, in Jesus's name," I said.

The nun eased the door a little more open but didn't relax her gaze. "Who are you?" she demanded. "How do you come to be here?"

"It's a long tale," I replied in haste. "The shorter part is that—coming from England—we were struck by a storm, the ship all but destroyed. We reached land only to have our father die. Somewhere south of here. Since then we've been wandering, trying to leave this land. Forgive us, Sister, but . . . we don't know where we are."

She considered my words in silence. "Are you," she asked, "trying to return to England?"

"To Iceland."

Her eyes narrowed. "I've never heard of such a place."

Troth sighed. My heart sank. All I could say was "If it pleases, Sister, we're in great need of food. Bread would be a blessing. Then we'll be happy to go on."

"Where was your home in England?" she asked.

"A tiny village," I said. "Not unlike this one. Called Stromford."

She gave no sign of recognition but said, "Tell me your names."

"Crispin," I said.

"And you?" she said to Troth.

When Troth shrank back, I said, "This is my sister, Troth."

The nun frowned. "Troth is not a Christian name."

"With permission, it's hers."

"Can't she speak for herself?"

"Her face has been broken since birth," I said. "She'd rather I speak for her."

The woman considered Troth again before turning back to me. "To whom do you belong?" she asked.

I tried to stand tall. "No one."

"You're too young for that," she snapped. "Have you run away?"

"We haven't!" I cried; and when she made no reply, I said, "It's true by all that's holy. Forgive me, Sister, we're very hungry. We haven't eaten in two days."

"Did the people in the village give you anything?"

I shook my head.

"Strangers are rare here," she said, her voice somewhat softer. "They hate the English. Her soldiers have come through this area and destroyed much."

"Sister," I pleaded, "we've nothing to do with such things."

The nun pursed her lips. Then she said, "Very well. You may come in." She held the door open.

"Begging your pardon, Sister," I said. "Will you give us some food?"

"My name is Sister Catherine," she said, her voice becoming hard again, her eyes glowering. "I am the hosteler of our convent. It's my duty to provide for guests."

Leaving the door open, she disappeared into the darkness as if to leave the choice to us.

Troth and I looked at each other.

"We'd best go in," I said, starting forward.

Troth stood her ground. "Crispin—she knows nothing of Iceland."

"She has food. . . ."

"But—"

I gave Troth an encouraging pull, and we stepped inside. Once we did, Sister Catherine slipped behind us and locked the door.

3

WE HAD STEPPED into a small room. Candlelight revealed walls paneled with old wood and a floor set with small stones. Opposite where we entered was another pair of closed doors. Against one wall was a bench. Over it was a wooden cross.

"In this convent," said the nun, continuing to study us as if we were a great curiosity, "we live mostly in silence.

We ask you to honor that as best you may. But it's also our rule to extend hospitality to guests, to help the needy, and to feed the poor.

"Therefore," she continued, "you will most likely be allowed to stay the night. But it's not for me to decide. I must consult our abbess. I'll see if she's awake. She's been ill. Stay here," she said, indicating the bench.

Without waiting for our response, the nun passed through the inner doors, taking the candle with her, leaving us in darkness. We heard her turn a lock behind her.

We felt about for the bench and sat side by side. My stomach grumbled with hunger.

"What is a convent?" Troth whispered.

"A church house," I said, remembering how little Troth knew of the world. "For women."

"What do they do here?"

I thought for a bit. "I'm not sure."

We sat there, waiting. "Crispin," Troth said shortly, "what if Iceland doesn't exist?"

"Bear said it does," I said, not wanting to admit how much the nun's words troubled me, too. "What we need now is food." We continued to wait.

Troth said, "Did you see the herbs growing by the path?"

"No."

"It was all overgrown, but I think it was once a garden," she said. "I'm sure I saw some curing herbs."

It was the kind of thing Troth would notice. I was trying to sit still, musing on what kind of food the nun might bring and if we'd be allowed to stay the night.

From somewhere deep within the building, a bell clanged. It was followed by the sound of soft steps beyond the inner door. Not long after—at a distance—we heard women singing. The voices were high, clear, and solemn. Though I could not understand the words, the sound softened the dark.

The inner door lock shifted and the door opened. Sister Catherine, her face illuminated by a lantern, reappeared.

"I have spoken to our abbess, Mother Marie," she announced. "As I told you, she's ill and in the infirmary. As is her custom, she wishes to see our visitors. Come." She put a finger to her lips. "Don't talk."

It was like following a shadow as we passed down a stone-paved corridor. Since the nun carried the only light, we saw little save columns and walls, all of stone. Here and there candles burned in cold niches.

The singing stopped. A bell rang. The only sound was our steps. Sister Catherine pushed a door open and made a motion with her hand. We stepped into a small room, its high ceiling lost in vaulted darkness. In one corner of the floor was a dish in which a small candle burned. Its trembling light revealed a wall covered with pictures. As I would later learn, the pictures depicted Saint Margaret's life and martyrdom.

Against another wall was a long table on which sat jars. There were also five narrow beds. Over each bed—on the wall—was affixed a small cross.

In one of the beds lay a woman. Propped up by pillows, wrapped in blankets, she seemed slight. Her thin, white face, encased by a dark shawl, had high cheekbones. Her eyes, ringed by darkness, were closed. The lines about her clenched mouth suggested pain. For a moment I was not even sure she was alive.

"Our abbess," Sister Catherine whispered. "Mother Marie."

Sitting in a chair next to the bedridden woman was another nun. Her head was bowed over a small blue-bound book that was cradled in her hands. Near her a second candle burned in a shallow bowl. As we approached, this nun did not look up but stood and stepped noiselessly to one side. She remained there as long as we did, eyes cast down, never speaking.

Sister Catherine bent over the woman in the bed. *"Mère Marie,"* she said softly, *"les enfants sont ici."*

The abbess shifted slightly and partly opened her eyes. At a touch from Sister Catherine, Troth and I stood before her.

"Bienvenue à notre abbaye," the sick nun said in a soft, husky voice. Her mouth twitched as if trying to smile. She did not have all her teeth.

"She welcomes you," Sister Catherine translated.

"Thank you," I said.

"Pardonnez-moi. Je suis malade."

"'Forgive me. I am ill'" came the translation.

The abbess spoke, and again Sister Catherine translated. "She says, 'It is our mission—in Mary's name—to be kind to poor strangers. You shall be fed and you may sleep here tonight.'"

Troth suddenly said, "What ails you?"

That Troth spoke at all startled me. It wasn't her way, since her garbled speech was hard for others to follow. Indeed, Sister Catherine looked at me in puzzlement. I repeated Troth's question so she could understand.

After a moment's hesitation, Troth's words were translated for the abbess. Mother Marie—looking only at Troth—replied in French. Sister Catherine translated.

"She has pains in her head."

"Where?" said Troth.

"Behind her eyes."

The abbess continued to gaze at Troth. Under such scrutiny, Troth normally stepped back. This time she remained in place. Nor did she cover her face with her hair as she always did when someone looked directly at her.

Troth and the abbess contemplated each other for a while. Then the sick nun took her thin arm out from beneath her blankets and extended her small hand. Troth stepped forward and grasped the hand.

Sister Catherine gasped.

I too was surprised.

For a moment the abbess and Troth remained with fingers linked. Neither spoke. Then the old nun, breathing deeply, pulled her hand away and closed her eyes. Her hand went back beneath the blankets.

Before I could speak, Troth said, "Thank you."

Sister Catherine touched her on the shoulder, then gathered me and guided us both out of the room.

Once outside, Sister Catherine said, "Follow me. I'll find you some food." Though I was sure she was unaware how rare it was for Troth to speak out or act as she had done, she kept glancing at her.

As the nun walked down long passageways, we stayed

close. Since we had left the infirmary, we had seen no one. Once the sister paused and pointed into the darkness. "Our church is there."

All I could see was some colored glass. The colors, illuminated from within, seemed to ripple like the surface of a flowing brook.

We were taken into what appeared to be another building, then a kitchen. It had two large ovens as well as open hearths in which smoldering red coals were piled. The room was warm and smelled of food. On a large, heavy table stood great pots and a pile of bread loaves. Sister Catherine gave us each a loaf. "We're allowed one pound of bread a day," she said. From a pot, she ladled tepid soup into two wooden bowls.

Troth suddenly said, "What does 'laide' mean?"

"'Ugly.' Why do you ask?"

Troth shook her head.

The nun looked at me for an explanation.

I only said, "A word she heard."

Once again Sister Catherine bade us to come. Holding on to our food, we were led into a corridor. On one side was a wall; the other side had a row of columns. Atop each column—half in shadow, half in lanternlight—I could see the sculpted heads of people. They seemed to be watching us.

Sister Catherine opened a door to a small room. "For our guests," she said.

Moonlight seeping through the two high windows revealed a bare room with three pallets of straw upon a stone floor. A crisscrossing timbered roof was overhead. On one wall was a flaking image of Saint Christopher carrying the infant Jesus on his back.

"You may sleep here," said Sister Catherine. "There's a blanket on each pallet."

"Thank you," I said.

Taking the lantern with her, Sister Catherine turned away. She was just about to leave the room when Troth called out, "I can cure that woman."

4

ISTER CATHERINE HALTED. "What did she say?"

I repeated Troth's words.

"Explain what she means." Though the command was put to me, Troth answered for herself.

"I know about plants and herbs," she said. "For healing."
I repeated her words so Sister Catherine could understand.

"How did you learn?"

"I was taught . . . by my mother."

"Where is your mother?"

"She died. But," said Troth, "she was a healer. A good one."

Sister Catherine lifted her lantern a little higher and considered Troth anew.

"Who takes care of your abbess?" Troth asked.

"We pray for her every day," said Sister Catherine. Then she added, "For a long time, we've had no infirmarian."

"What's an infirmarian?" Troth asked.

"The one who cares for us if we become ill. How might you help her?"

"For the ailment your lady has, a drink of feverfew leaves and chamomile could help."

Sister Catherine stared at her.

"They are herbs," Troth explained.

"I know what they are!" the nun snapped. "Where would you find such things?"

"As we came along your path," said Troth, "I saw feverfew. If I look for chamomile, I'll find it. It's common."

Sister Catherine, her lips pursed, her brow furrowed,

remained quiet for a moment. "In the morning," she said, "I'll speak to the abbess."

With a sudden swirl of her black robe she left the room, leaving us in darkness.

Troth and I sat on the floor, and in such light as the moon cast through the windows, devoured the food we'd been given.

"They make good bread," I said, gobbling it down.

Troth said nothing.

"Perhaps they'll let us stay for a few days," I went on. "We could offer to do some work. It'll be worth it for the food. And maybe someone here knows where Iceland is."

"Crispin," said Troth, "I really can help that sick woman!"

I looked around. "Are you sure?"

"Aude used to say we must always try."

I shrugged and swallowed the rest of my bread.

While Troth remained sitting some distance from me with her back against a wall, I lay down on one of the straw pallets and drew the wool blanket over me. Its warm comfort made me realize how tired I was. As I lay there, it occurred to me that I had not slept under a roof since Rye. I told myself not to get used to such luxury. I suspected we still had a long way to go.

I shifted and was about to ask Troth what she thought of Sister Catherine. My friend was staring intently out one of the windows, toward the moon. Wondering what she was thinking, I watched her for a while until, overcome by great tiredness, I slept.

Ringing bells woke me at dawn. I sat up and looked around. By the soft light, I could see that Troth was still asleep.

The door creaked open. Sister Catherine looked in. "Morning prayers," she announced. "Prime. You must come." She waited.

I gave Troth a little shake. She sat and rubbed her eyes, looked at Sister Catherine, but said nothing.

Once again we went with the nun. She led us to their church and had us stand at the back of the nave, by the entrance. Hanging lanterns and candles let me see it wasn't a very big church. The ceiling was vaulted, with interlacing tracery. Windows were high and small. Some, as I had noticed, were colored. Walls had pictures on them, but it was too gloomy for me to see what they were. The air smelled of old incense.

Leaving us, Sister Catherine joined the other nuns, who sat in facing rows during the mass. At the altar stood a priest, an open book before him. Speaking in Latin, he offered the mass. Now and again the sisters chanted and sang. Bells rang.

When the service was done, the nuns filed out in silence, heads slightly bowed, hands clasped, their faces white against their dark robes. Though they passed near us, I didn't see any of them look in our direction, not once.

The day was brightening as Sister Catherine guided us back to the kitchen. This time I could see that many of the walls had colorful images and painted sculpture.

In the kitchen people were at work preparing food. They did not appear to be nuns. Rather, they seemed to be servants, who glanced at us disapprovingly. Sister Catherine ordered that bread be given us.

Our hands full, the nun guided us away. I soon realized she was bringing us to the entryway. Troth guessed it, too. She reached out and tugged at Sister Catherine's sleeve. Surprised, the woman turned.

"Did you tell your sick lady I could help her?" asked Troth.

Sister Catherine looked at me for understanding. I repeated Troth's words. The nun studied Troth for a long while, as if trying to make up her mind. In the end she said, "Come with me, the both of you." She chose a new direction.

I now saw other nuns. They walked briskly, paying us no attention. No one spoke. The silence was something one could almost feel.

We returned to the infirmary. The abbess was in her bed, eyes closed. In her hands was a rosary, over which her fingers flitted. Her thin lips moved slightly.

Sister Catherine went to the bedside. Whispering, she said, *"Mère Marie. La jeune fille est ici."*

The abbess opened her eyes and gazed at us. She made a movement with her hand, which drew Sister Catherine close. The nun listened to something the abbess said, then stood and turned to me. "You must come with me. Your sister will stay."

I turned to Troth.

She nodded.

Wondering what would happen to Troth, I was led back to the kitchen. When we entered, the women stopped their work and looked at us.

"Mettez ce garçon au travail," Sister Catherine ordered, and left.

One of the women came up to me. She must have realized I didn't speak French. All she did was pull at my arm and lead me to a great stone basin, into which cold water was flowing. Nearby was a great pile of wooden bowls and iron pots.

I spent the morning working, my hands chafed by cold water and rubbing sand. I spent most of the time thinking about Troth, wondering what was happening, what she was doing, if she could help the nun.

It was not until the afternoon that Troth and I were reunited. I was already in the sleeping room. When she came, she brought more bread and bowls of some meat stew. A rare treat. Her movements were quick, her eyes full of life. I hadn't seen her so for a long time. And yet she didn't speak.

While I ate slowly, she bolted her food down. "What happened?" I finally asked.

"The abbess said that her pain was great," she related. "It sits behind her eyes and keeps her from her prayers. She asked if I thought I could truly help her. I told her I could, with an infusion of feverfew and chamomile. I had to speak slowly so Sister Catherine could understand me, since she was translating for us. Then the abbess asked me if I was a Christian. I said I didn't know. Then she asked me where I came from. I told her about my life. About Aude. How Aude died. She said she would have the sisters pray for her. She even offered *me* a blessing. Crispin," said Troth, her eyes bright. "She looks upon me with kindness. She . . . she's not frightened of my face. And," Troth concluded with a bright smile, "she said she would let me try and cure her pains."

It was good to see her so happy. I said, "What do you need to do?"

"I know where feverfew is growing. It's the chamomile we need to find."

A different nun led us to the main doors. She gave Troth a small basket. Though the nun showed no interest in me, she kept glancing at Troth. Not that she spoke.

Outside—in great contrast to the dim convent—it was a bright, sharp day, the clouds high, the sky a deep blue. With Troth leading the way, we went behind the buildings into the woods. She fairly skipped along, while I came slowly. Her elation was making me ill at ease because I wasn't part of it. It made me restless, too, and I wished we would leave this place and go on our way.

Every now and again, Troth would pause and examine some plant, then rub it between her fingers and smell it. Then she'd announce, "Here's myrtle. That's for bad joints." Or, "Here's lily of the valley. For clearing thoughts. Crispin, there's so much here I can use. I think all these things were planted here." She laughed. "Maybe they were set here by the infirmarian as an excuse to go wandering in the woods. To get out of that silent place. These woods are full of noise."

In late afternoon she found a flowery plant growing by a large boulder. She picked it and made me smell it.

"Do you like it?" Her eyes were smiling.

"It's strong. What is it?"

She grinned. "Chamomile."

As we headed back to the convent, Troth chatted blithely. "Many of the plants Aude taught me about are here. I saw marigold—good for wounds. And parsley. It's used for many things. I'll have to search more."

Her words made me increasingly uneasy. "What if your potion doesn't cure the nun?"

"I think it will." She sounded confident.

Returning to the convent, I used the knocker to gain entry. Another nun opened the door. She must have known of us, for she let us in without speaking and took us directly to the room where we had slept. But as soon as we got there, she made motions with her hands that indicated Troth should go with her. She made it equally clear I was to remain behind.

Annoyed and frustrated, I stayed in the room for a long time. In my heart, I admitted I didn't want Troth's cure to work. If it did—the thought came—maybe they would want her to stay. I wanted us to go.

When Troth returned, she told me how she had made

the infusion and given it to the abbess.

"Did it work?"

"We'll have to see."

Though I spent a restless night, Troth slept well.

In the morning it was not the bells that woke us but a hard knock on the door. When I opened the door, it was Sister Catherine.

For the first time, I saw her smile. "Mother Marie's pains have lessened."

An excited Troth, all but skipping, went away with her. My time was spent in the kitchen, where I cleaned things and hauled wood and water. No one spoke to me. I chafed at the time and the work, wishing Troth would come back, wondering where she was.

I did not see her again until I was taken to church for vespers. We stood side by side in the back. "Where were you?" I whispered.

"They asked me to see other nuns," she said.

"What for?"

"Their ailments. One sister has a bad elbow. Another has a red eye."

"Can you help them?"

She smiled shyly.

After the service the nuns filed past us as before. This

time I saw many glances in our direction—all toward Troth. They knew what she had done.

5

HE THIRD DAY was much like the second. My time, as before, was spent doing tasks in the kitchen. Troth was away from me all day. I felt very alone. At one point when I carried in some wood, I was able to wander a bit about the convent and look upon the many images on the walls. I think they depicted different saints and how they found their martyrdom. There were devils, too, as well as beasts in strange and wonderful shapes.

And there were columns everywhere, made of heavy stone and ornamented with leaves, crosses, and symbols I didn't understand.

As it turned out, Troth had visited nuns who were ill or who had pains. Then she had gone—alone—in search of herbs and plants.

"Why didn't you ask me to come with you?" I asked

when we were finally together again.

"I was able to find what I needed," she said. "Crispin, the old infirmarian really had a good garden. It just needs tending." She looked at me. I must have shown how I felt. "They told me you were busy," she added gently. Abruptly she snatched my hand and kissed it.

I was somewhat soothed, but still worried.

That night, after mass, Sister Catherine brought us back to our sleeping room where we were meant to eat. The nun started to leave, only to pause at the door as if making a decision. Quite suddenly, she turned back toward us and started to speak. It took effort for her to do so, and she often paused between words, as if struggling to climb a steep way. She seemed to be addressing Troth more than me.

"I was brought here," she began, her voice low, "when I was a girl. Young, like you. Left here when my father went off to the wars. He promised that when his obligation to his lord was done, he would bring me home to England. I waited and waited, but . . . he never returned. I thought he had been killed. So of course I prayed for him and remained."

She cleared her throat and put a hand to her chest as if it hurt. "Some time later, I discovered that when he'd left me, he had paid the dowry fee. So that I would stay. He . . . he had never intended to return."

I saw tears in her eyes.

"It can be hard here sometimes," the nun continued. "And lonely. No one else speaks English. But then we speak but rarely. We do learn Latin. We study sacred texts. My sisters—there are thirty-two of us—are, for the most part, kind and loving. I try to serve Jesus and Mary with all my faith and heart that I might become perfect in Their eyes. Though I have times of great joy, there is much bitterness in me. Our abbess often reminds me of something Saint Cyril said: 'If you can go no farther than where you are, God has shown you your destiny.'"

For a moment she stood in silence. Then she went on: "In all the time I've been here—I can no longer tell how long—our abbess has never taken my hand the way she did yours. Our rule says we are not to touch one another."

She left the room quickly.

"Why did she tell you that?" I demanded.

Troth looked away. I waited. She finally faced me. "They wish me to stay here."

My heart lurched. "Why?" I asked, though I knew the answer.

"As their infirmarian."

I swallowed. "Will you?"

She turned from me again. "I don't know."

I was not sure I believed her. "And be like Sister Catherine?"

She looked at me fiercely. "She *had* to stay. If I remain, it's because I choose to."

Too upset to argue, I went to my pallet and lay down, my back toward her.

I was woken in the middle of the night by the bells. Prime prayers. Drowsy, I sat up and looked around. The moonlight seeping through the windows was as cold as the air. I shifted on my pallet, ready to go back to sleep, when I realized I hadn't seen Troth. Sleepiness fell from me. I sat up and looked about. She was gone.

Alarmed, I got up. I pushed the door open and stepped into the long and gloomy walkway. It was open to the air, colder than the room. Looking up, I could see a glow of light—red and blue—seeping through the church windows.

Standing where I was, the moonlight allowed me to see the far end of the corridor. I saw some nuns in a line, moving away from me. Save for their shuffling feet, they made no sound. As I watched, their black gowns folded into the darkness. I supposed they were going to the church and wondered if Troth was with them. Should I follow? I was not sure what to do.

I stood still and listened. Wind slid through the corridor and caused a leaf to grate along the floor stones. Bells rang. Chanting began. I didn't want to hear it. Didn't want to go to the church.

Instead, I looked into an open space, toward what appeared to be some kind of garden. In the very center of the space was a statue, of whom I could not tell. There were also a few benches. It took me a while to realize that Troth was sitting on one of them, her blanket around her shoulders. She was leaning back, hands propping her up from behind. She seemed to be staring at the stars.

I made my way to where she sat.

"Troth . . . ?"

Startled, she turned.

"It's me. Crispin. Are you all right?"

"I'm fine."

When she said no more, I said, "What . . . what are you doing?"

"Wishing Aude would talk to me." Her voice was full of yearning.

"Aude!"

"I need her to tell me what to do."

I began to feel afraid. "About . . . what?" I asked.

"Should I go on . . . or stay?"

It took me a moment before I could speak. "Why would you want to stay?"

"I could help these people—like Aude helped others."

I could not reply. At length I found my voice and said, "But what . . . what about Iceland?"

At first she did not answer. Then she said, "We don't know where it is. What . . . what if we can't get there?"

"We will," I insisted.

"It's not so sure."

"We promised Bear—"

"We never promised. We decided on our own. Besides," she said softly, "he's gone. He can't help us."

Struggling against the pain I felt in my chest, I took a deep breath and said, "And . . . me?"

She didn't answer.

"And me?" I repeated louder. I was becoming panicky.

"You are my dearest friend. But . . ."

"But . . . what?"

"I need to think. Maybe this is where I should be."

All I could say was "It's cold out here."

"I'll come soon."

I stood there for a while, but when Troth made no

movement and said no more, I made my way back to the sleeping room. Just as I stepped through the door, I saw the nuns returning. Feeling a swell of anger, I hurried inside.

I lay down on my pallet and drew the blanket up. I could not sleep. My heart ached too much. I kept thinking what I would do if Troth remained. This wasn't the freedom I wanted.

I could not, would not stay in the kitchen. But I could not see where else I could work in this women's place. I couldn't stay in the village.

The question Did I truly wish to leave? flooded in on me. It had been so long since I'd been alone. Not since I'd met Bear. True, before I knew him, being alone was most of my life. But I knew so little then! I had changed. I had come to love others: Bear, Troth, Aude, the people in Rye. I had a bitter thought: The more love you have for others, the more pain there is in losing them.

Why must seeking my freedom be so painful?

I waited for Troth, but though I lay awake a long time, she did not come.

6

HEN I WOKE in the morning, the first thing I did was to look for Troth. To my great relief, she was there on her pallet, sleeping.

I wanted to wake her, impatient to learn if she had made a decision. At the same time, I feared knowing what her choice might be. When she finally woke, I didn't know what to say or ask, so said nothing.

She lay on her side, her large, dark eyes watching me. I could hardly look at her. But when I did, I was sure I understood. She was trying to show sadness. I didn't believe it. "You're going to stay here, aren't you?" I blurted out.

"They need me."

"I need you!"

"Not as much." She sat up. "You're angry."

"If I said I was going to leave you, how would you feel?"

"Sad."

"I'll be alone," I pleaded, though I knew it was useless.

"You'll always have me," she said softly. "And Bear. In your thoughts."

"But not by my side." I wiped tears from my face.

"In your heart," she added.

"And . . . yours?" I said, barely able to speak.

"Always."

"If you stay," I asked her, "would you become one of them?"

"I don't know."

"But why stay here?" I cried.

She came and knelt before me. Took up my hand. "Crispin, I want to be where I'm needed." She spoke evenly, with sureness. "Where I can do the things Aude taught me to do. To learn more. And Crispin, it's quiet here. Protected. They will accept me for what I am. I can be happy. I can be free here. I . . . don't have to hide my face."

"I . . . love your face."

She threw her arms around me and hugged me tightly.

"I want you to go," she said.

"Why?"

"This place isn't for you. Going to Iceland is what you want to do. Isn't it?"

I could only nod.

We remained with our arms around each other for a long time.

"May God keep you," I whispered. "I'll go."

I remained at the convent for two more days. Even that

was far more than I wished. I wanted to leave immediately. To run away. All the same, I did not want to leave. I was fearful. Uneasy. Sometimes angry. How can you miss someone before you leave them?

As for Troth, though she tried not to show it, she was full of joy. That joy was wormwood to me. I tried to take pleasure in it, but it was too hard. Painful.

The night before I was to leave, we slept but little. Instead, we talked for many hours. We spoke of the time when she first found Bear and me in the forest. What she thought of me, and I her. How she and Aude had taken us in and treated Bear's wounds. We spoke of Aude's ghastly death. Our flight to Rye. The kind family there of which we became a part. Bear's fondness for the widow Benedicta. Our sudden flight and the stormy voyage to France on the cog. How Bear died. Our wanderings. In all, I understood how much Bear and then Troth had become root and flower of my life.

"I wish we had stayed in Rye," I said. "We would have had a large family."

"But you shall go to Iceland," she said.

"Maybe it's as Sister Catherine said: 'If you can go no farther than where you are, God has shown you your destiny.'"

She snatched up my hand and gave it many kisses. "Promise me you'll go!" she cried. "So I'll always know where you are."

I attempted to smile. "What if I can't find it?"

"You will."

"I'll . . . try."

She smiled. "Maybe . . . maybe I won't know where your feet are. But I'll always know where your heart is."

Then we embraced each other again and cried.

Not wishing to burden Troth with more of my sorrow, I slipped away by early dawn, while the sisters were at their prayers. Troth was already with them. I could hear their sweet, chorused voices.

Clutching a sack of food that Sister Catherine had provided, I closed the convent doors behind me. Once outside I took a deep, if broken, breath. My eyes were full of tears. The air was cold and damp, thick with a promise of rain. Below me, the wretched village lay in darkness. Beyond the convent, I seemed to be the only stirring soul.

Much of my heart wished to stay with Troth and go no farther. But she had made her choice; and for the love I bore her, I knew that I must respect it—hard as it was. She could be free here.

More than anything, I wished to go on to Iceland.

Briefly I strove to imagine what my freedom would be like. What I saw—in my mind—were people full of good grace and cheer and little fearfulness, hard at work in fields of tall, ripe grain. By going there—I told myself—I would show Troth that I could be part of a world that was good and fruitful.

So it was that after making the sign of the cross over my heart, I stepped away, once more heading northward.

I still had little idea where to go. But wishing to be alone in my thoughts, I chose as isolated a path as I could find. No fingerposts or milestones for me. By the time the rising sun cast a red sheen upon the overcast clouds, I was well gone.

I was sure I had left my heart behind.

7

Y MIDMORNING ON that first day, cold, gray rain began to fall. No passing squall, either, but rain that stopped and started for many days, turning the paths I followed into

running streams clotted with mud and leaves. In all of this, my torn and wet clothing proved useless. My body ached. As for the bread I'd been given, it was gone so quickly my stomach hurt as if it never knew the swell of food.

I did try to hunt, but whether it was the wretched weather or my inept skills, I failed completely. All I could find to eat were shriveled berries, bitter to the tongue. And I was dreadfully lonely.

No wonder, then, that with every step I took, I half believed Iceland would be around each turning. My resolve was made of equal parts stubbornness and hope, the kind of hope that confuses desire with reality.

But when the rains finally ceased and the weather cleared, it only turned colder. Songbirds fled. I saw no game. The biting air hurt my ears and chin. When—rare event—I met someone, I still had no language to share and could gain no knowledge of where I was or how best to go on. The word *Iceland* appeared to mean nothing to people.

Though my faith in Bear's knowledge remained absolute, I lacked all notions as to which way to turn, what I should or *could* do. My resolve weakened. While I missed Troth greatly, I took comfort in thinking her secure and was glad she had stayed behind. It would have driven me mad to have her share my hopelessness, even while trusting me to find us safety. Nonetheless, my heart cried out for some welcome in the unloving world. I began to think I'd been a fool to go on alone, that it would have been better to drudge in that convent kitchen than perish in this cold wilderness. If I had known the way back, I would have gone.

After any number of days passed in such a fashion, I became convinced I must forgo all hopes of Iceland. For the moment, I turned my thoughts to Rye and the family of which we had been a brief part. Might not they take me in again, if not for my own sake, then for the love of Bear? The idea was balm until I had to admit I had no more knowledge of how to get to Rye than to Iceland.

In short, after so many days of wasted wanderings and useless musings, I was as adrift as a dismasted ship upon the open sea.

Utterly lost and friendless, I stumbled off the narrow forest path I'd been blindly following. What was the point, I asked myself, of going any farther? For all I knew, I was going *away* from my goal.

I roamed through the forest until, empty of tears and devoid of strength, I gave way to my exhaustion. Surrounded by the creaks and cracks of the darkling night, I huddled upon the ground while overhead a pale moon shrouded all in sickly light. Then a whipping wind began to lay siege to me, swirling so, it stripped last leaves from trees, turning them into shivering skeletons—much like me. Chilled to my very marrow, I blew upon my fingers in hopes I might catch some heat.

I was too alone, worn, and hungry, and I grew colder every moment. Knowing winter had barely begun, my need to find shelter, food, and human company could not have been greater.

Sitting there, now and again crying, I began to think I'd not live for very long. Trying to prepare myself, I sought comfort in thoughts of Bear and Troth, even of Old Aude. I thought of that wretched cook I'd killed and begged his forgiveness for what I'd done. I whispered pleading prayers to my patron, the blessed Saint Giles, seeking his intercession that God might forgive my sins and touch me with some tender mercy.

Then, unexpectedly, from out of the shadowy forest came a shrill and ghastly shriek. Its high skirling made me think the worst: that some devil was crying for my blood.

The very next moment, the dreadful sound completely changed. I began to hear the sweet voices of many musical strands. The change was as shocking as when I first heard the ghastly noise. It was as if some evil thing, having shamelessly announced itself, now masked its face in sacred song, and that music wrapped about me soothingly, enticingly.

Was it, I wondered, the sound of descending angels, a miraculous gift from my Saint Giles? I recalled that it was music that first led me to Bear. Perhaps here, too, the music might be coming from kindly people. That's to say, though at first I'd been greatly frightened, I quickly convinced myself that here was rescue. If these were people with food, by Saint Jude, I would be saved.

With the music drawing me like some enchantment, I stumbled about the woods in hopes of discovering from where it came. It wasn't long before I spied a small flame among the trees. Added to the light was a whiff of roasting food.

Oh, how my stomach spoke!

Not bothering to suppress the sound of my steps, I charged through the woods. I soon drew near enough to observe five people sitting by a fire: two men, two women, and a boy. All were wrapped in cloaks, hoods thrown back. Four sat together on one side of the fire, while the older of the women—she had a long gray braid down her back—sat on the other. Between them they had set up a crude spit over a fire. Two birds were roasting, their oozing fat making the flames sizzle and snap while sending out mouthwatering smells.

The boy was playing the small drum some called a naker. The others were playing a harp, a mandola, and a bagpipe. As soon as I saw the bagpipe, I realized it was its sound that I'd first heard. Shrill, to be sure, but nothing fiendish.

The older woman who sat opposite the four had no instrument. Rather, she was leading the four in their music making by singing in a high, wavering voice while jigging one foot up and down to set the tune.

Near the boy lay what appeared to be a ragged ball of fur. And within easy reach of the men was a sword as well as a large blade. The flame's sparkling light made their edges gleam. These weapons—I told myself—were no more than I would wish for defense in such a wild place. Here was safety, too.

In short, it was all I desired: company, warmth, food, and security.

As I stood there, transfixed, the woman singer, with a wave of her hand, abruptly changed their music from a plain tune to one of greater liveliness. It was a melody of great cheer, so very like what I had played while Bear had danced.

My heart leaped with joy and made it impossible for me to think any ill of these people. Quite the opposite. At that moment I had no concern who they were or why they were there—only that they would offer me a welcome.

With my heart fluttering like a small bird, I stepped forward to show myself.

<h1 style="text-align:center">8</h1>

HOUGH I DIDN'T SEEK to hide the sound of my steps, the musicians were so engaged in their playing that even when I stood at the edge of their encampment, they failed to notice me. Instead, it was the ball of fur at the boy's feet which— to my complete astonishment—came to life, revealing himself as a tiny, furry man! His ugly, distorted face, offering a most hideous, toothy grin, glared at me, and then he began to screech horribly.

The younger woman spun about. When she saw me standing there, she cried, "Mother of God!"

Equally startled, the other musicians turned, saw me, and instantly stopped their playing. The harp player snatched at a leather sack that lay at his feet and thrust it behind him. The bearded man flung his bagpipe down, plucked the sword from the ground, sprang up, and pointed the blade toward me.

"Peace be with you!" I cried in haste.

The little man leaped upon the boy's chest and clung to him, even as he twisted his head around and grimaced at me fiercely. To my further bewilderment, I saw he had a tail!

It was the gray-haired woman—the one who had been singing and leading the music—who lifted a hand to calm the man with the sword.

"In the name of Jesus," she called out tensely, "who are you?"

God knows I must have been an outlandish sight. To see me step out unexpectedly from the forest as I had done would have upset the stoutest heart.

But on my part, what I felt beyond all else was vast relief that they spoke English. "My name . . ." I stammered, even as I offered an inept bow, "is . . . Crispin. I'm lost and hungry. Your fire and music led me to you. I mean no harm."

I waited tensely for some reply since, as if unsure, the five continued to study me in silence. As I stood there, my eyes went to the strange little creature, wondering what he was.

The gray-haired woman stood. Her face was old, with

small eyes, a sharp nose and chin, and a puckered mouth. Though not much taller than I, she had a commanding stance. With her head tilted slightly to one side and her arms akimbo, I felt challenged.

"But what are you doing here?" she demanded, her voice bold and loud as though from a larger person.

"Forgive me, mistress. It's a long tale," I replied, and gave a swift version of my tale: that I came from England, was storm wrecked, and had lost my father. That I had been wandering ever since, trying to leave this land, but had become lost.

"Where were you hoping to go?" asked the bearded man.

"If it pleases . . . to Iceland."

As if puzzled, they looked at one another.

"Don't . . . don't you know where it is?" I asked.

"Only that it must be a cold place," said the younger man, smiling slightly as if pleased with his jest. "But, as Saint Gerard is my witness, I've never heard of it."

"Nor I," said the bearded man.

But the younger woman said, "I think . . . I think I have."

We all looked to her.

"Where is it?" challenged the bearded man.

The woman shrugged. "Far off. Beyond the sea."

My heart sank.

"Don't you think," the bearded man said to me, "it would be smarter to go to Calais?"

Knowing nothing of such a place, all I could say was "If it be wise."

"Your speech tells me it's England where you mean to go," said the gray-haired woman. "And Calais, which isn't far, is English. It offers the shortest sail home."

"Or perhaps to your . . . . land of ice," said the bearded man, smiling.

"Wherever is best," I said, eager to agree.

The older, bearded man, eyes agleam with firelight, asked, "How old are you?"

"Thirteen years, I think."

While the others waited for the gray-haired woman to speak, she studied me. Finally she said, "You said your father was killed. How did it happen?"

"In . . . in a battle."

"May the Mother of God keep your father's soul," she murmured, her face softening slightly as she made the sign of the cross over her chest.

The bearded man leaned in eagerly. "Was he a soldier?"

I shook my head. "We . . . we were wandering musicians."

"Musicians!" exclaimed the gray-haired woman, one eyebrow lifted. Then she smiled. "Truly?"

The man holding the sword lowered it a bit. "If you're a musician," asked the man who had been playing the harp, "how did you come to be in a battle?"

I said, "When my father and I came off our wrecked ship, free soldiers fell upon us. They forced us to join them."

"Those soldiers are hateful," agreed the younger woman. "All they do is murder and plunder."

A silence, broken by the snap of the fire, followed as they continued to study me. Of the five, only the dirty-faced boy had not spoken. He just stared at me, his mouth agape, now and again wiping his runny nose with the back of his hand.

One of the men called out, "You call yourself a musician. What instrument do you play?"

"The recorder."

"Excellent! Show it to us."

I made an ungainly bow. "Forgive me, masters. It was lost at sea."

"A musician without his instrument," said the gray-haired woman, "is like a priest without his cross."

"And makes," I beseeched, "for a hungry soul."

She smiled. "Have you nothing, then?"

I held out my empty hands. "By blessed Saint Anthony, all I had was lost. What you see is," I said, struggling to suppress the tightness in my chest, "is . . . . all I am."

The woman glanced at her companions. They may have communicated something with a nod, or a look, which I did not see—or perhaps the woman made up her own mind. She turned back to me and said, "My name is Elena. Of London, England. This is my family. We too are wandering musicians. You're welcome to share what food we have. Perhaps God sent you. We lack a recorder player—and," she said with a quick glance toward the others, "if you prove honest—we might find a use for you."

"Blessings on you for your welcome," I said, struggling to speak even as relief brought tears to my eyes.

"Come then," said the woman. "Give us your name again."

"Crispin."

"Crispin, then, without shoes," she said, turning to the others. "These are my two sons, Rauf and Gerard."

Rauf, the one who held the sword, appeared to be the elder of the brothers. Squat and broad shouldered, he had a heavy, black-bearded face. Dirty, matted hair stuck out from under an old red cloth cap, which he wore low on his forehead. He had a distrustful cast to his half-lidded eyes, as if peeping out from behind some ill-fitting mask. On his brow was a scar, new enough to be red with mending. It matched his surly, ill-tempered look. He walked, as I would discover, with a limp. It was he who had been playing the bagpipe.

His brother, Gerard, was as great a contrast to the angelic instrument he held—the harp—as one might ever see. Somewhat taller than his brother, but not so big in bulk, he too had dark hair, with a rough, pock-marked face and a smile that showed large teeth. His eyes shifted often, as if seeking approval from the others for what he said. More than anyone, he looked to his older brother.

Elena continued. "Rauf's wife, Woodeth."

Woodeth was a buxom woman, short and thick, with fair, if dirty, hair and a weathered, coarse face that had suffered a broken nose. She kept her lips tightly compressed, perhaps to hide the gaps in her teeth. The mandola was in her lap.

"Our servant boy, Owen," concluded Elena, indicating the boy.

This boy was small, younger than I, with dark curly hair, a pinched, filthy face with thin lips, and large, watery eyes that stared at me timidly. The torn clothing he wore did not hide the bruise marks on his arms. It was to this Owen that the little fur man clung.

Even as Elena introduced Owen, Rauf leaned over and slapped the boy on the head. Whether it was meant to be playful or not, the boy winced and shrank away, eyes cast down as if ashamed.

Now that I truly saw these people, they appeared, despite their cheerful music, a rough-cut clan. And beyond the fire's edge, I noticed other weapons besides the sword and blade. Which is to say, these people were heavily armed—more so, it occurred to me, than might be considered needful.

"As for that creature," Elena said, looking toward what I had thought to be a miniature man, "he's called a monkey."

"Is he not . . . human?"

"Not at all," said Elena.

"Can he speak?"

"Gibberish," said Rauf.

I stared.

"Mostly harmless," said Gerard. He leaned out and gave a sharp tug to the leather strip that held the beast. The monkey hissed at him.

"Though," added Rauf, "be advised: he has his temper, with teeth and claws. We call him Schim."

"Schim only obeys the boy," Elena went on, turning the attention back to me, "but the beast helps us greatly in our work. And it's our work," she went on, "that takes us to Calais. A Master Humfrey Talbot, a wealthy merchant in the wool trade there, is having a wedding for his daughter. Word has spread that he wishes musicians to attend. We hope to play at the festivities and earn enough to bring us safely home to England."

"Forgive my ignorance, mistress," I said. "But what manner of place is this Calais?"

"It's a fine walled city by the sea," explained Gerard. "As many, they say, as three thousand live there—plus an English garrison." He darted a glance at his brother for confirmation.

"Great King Edward," agreed Rauf, "took it from the French some years ago. Ever since, it's been under English rule. And better for it, I'm sure."

"A trading place," said Elena. "With much wealth."

"But mostly surrounded by the French," added Woodeth. "Which is not so good. It can make it hard to reach."

"Indeed," said Gerard with a glance at his brother, "we've been wondering how best to get there."

To this Elena quickly added, "But all sea merchants plying the English trade are required to pass through its port. Many ships go back and forth."

"So it will take no real effort," said Rauf, "for you to find your passage."

"God is kind," I replied.

"He has been to us," said Rauf with a quick, sly look at the others.

"But if you can make music," Elena was quick to add, "you should consider joining us."

"The richer the sound, the richer the reward," coaxed Gerard. "As Elena said, we've no one to play recorder."

"Not anymore," said Rauf with a knowing air. "Owen," he cried, kicking out upon the boy. "Fetch Master Mark's recorder."

Owen started up—the monkey still clinging to him—grabbed a sack, and pulled out a weathered recorder. He offered it to Rauf, but the instrument was waved on to me.

As I took it, I briefly wondered who Mark was and where he was now. More importantly, I knew I was being called upon to prove myself. Much, I thought, would depend on it.

With the recorder in my hands, silently blessing the day Bear taught me how to play, I fingered the holes. I raised the instrument to my lips, took breath, and played a simple song.

"'Ah, Dear God, How Can This Be,'" said Elena, naming the tune I'd offered. "We know it well."

They all nodded and seemed relieved that I'd been able to prove I was what I claimed to be.

I lay the recorder down and picked up three stones that lay at my feet. I began to juggle. That brought grins of delight. Even the boy gave a shy smile.

"A juggler, too!" cried Rauf. "Nothing could be better."

"Deft hands are always welcome in our trade," added a smirking Gerard with a quick look at the others, as if sharing a jest.

"We can do tricks, too," said Rauf. "Owen!" he cried. "Make Schim jump!"

The boy set the monkey down and said, "Jump!"—the first word I heard him say.

To my amazement, the creature did a complete somersault and then, grimacing, leaped back to the boy.

"Never mind the beast," said Elena. "Come, we'll make music until the birds are cooked."

This promise of food made me more willing than ever to find goodness in these people. "Hard looks," I had once heard Bear say, "can mask soft hearts."

Elena turned to her family. "In honor of our guest:

'The Jolly Juggler,'" she announced. With that she began to sing while the others played.

Once I gathered the sense of the tune, I took up the recorder anew and joined in, taking pleasure that I could. As I played, they looked at me and nodded, and then did so to one another. For his part, Schim the monkey walked—if that's the word—to Rauf, leaped up, and grabbed his red cap. Legs bowed, the creature waddled upright toward me, holding the cap before him as if begging. When I gave him nothing, he made a toothy expression, retreated, curled himself into a ball upon the boy's lap, and appeared to sleep.

But we played on. Though I did not truly know these people and they did not know me, the music formed a bond. It was as Bear had once told me, "Music is the only language to survive the curse of Babel."

For the first time since I had left Troth, I was calm. And what was even better, I felt safe.

9

HE MUSIC MAKING DONE, we finally supped. Even Schim, the monkey, received his bit. He held his portion in his tiny hands while continuing to stare at me. No doubt, I studied him as much.

While we ate, the whole family—save the boy, who remained silent the entire meal—talked of where they had been. They had been part of the Duke of Sunderland's retinue. They went with him from the English city of London to an Italian place called Genoa. Then the duke unexpectedly made for home, promising to return. He didn't. They never learned why.

Worse, they explained, the duke left them without any money. (Rauf cursed him roundly.) Abandoned, they had little choice but to try to make their way back to England as best they could. They had been doing so by performing at fairs and, when able, in the homes of merchants and noblemen. As the family traveled north from Genoa, they passed through Italian lands, over high mountains, and on into Gascony, to the wine city of Bordeaux.

"Where England's new boy king, Richard, was born," put in Gerard.

After months of travel, they were finally close to their London home. "Calais," said Elena, "is, we think, just a short march away."

From there they planned to sail for England and London, vowing never to venture across the seas again.

By then the food had made me relaxed. The fire had warmed me. Their easy talk was soothing. I felt much at my ease.

"But now, Master Crispin," Elena said to me, "it's your turn to tell us more of your travels."

"You said you and your father joined a band of soldiers," said Rauf, his eyes hard upon me. "Were you engaged in any fighting?"

The question seemed weighted with meanings I could not grasp. Not wishing to say anything that might cause them to turn me away, I wasn't sure how to answer.

"Fighting?" I echoed. "Not . . . directly."

"No experience with weapons?" Gerard asked.

I felt the heat of shame on my face. "May Jesus forgive me—I had to kill a man."

Rauf's eyes seemed full of eagerness. "Well now," he said with a knowing glance to the others. "How did a boy like you come to that?"

While I tried to think how best to reply, they leaned forward with anticipation. I could hardly escape the notion that they were pleased by what I, ashamed, had revealed.

"A man attacked me," I said, adding, "I . . . I had no choice."

"Ah!" cried Rauf, sitting back. "I can understand that."

When the others smiled and nodded, I was comforted by their sympathy.

"Have you no other family?" asked Woodeth.

"A sister."

"Where is she?"

"In . . . a convent."

That stilled them for a while. Then Elena said, "Share more of your life."

I felt obliged to tell them, though not my entire tale. But by Saint Anselm, what I said was true, save that Bear was not my real father.

Their faces intent, often nodding encouragement, now and again exchanging glances—as when I told them of Bear's death—they listened closely. The only one who moved was the boy, who went about and put the family's things—cloaks, bags, knives—in order like a mute servant. Now and again he stole a glance at me, but since he had spoken just that one word, I began to wonder if he could truly talk.

As for the monkey, he slept.

When I finally finished my tale, there was silence, broken only by the snap and spark of the dying fire and the sound of wind sifting through the trees. I felt rather like a fish hauled from safe waters that now lay floundering on the land. Would they keep me or throw me back?

Elena said, "Then there is no one to whom you are bound?"

Too full of emotion to speak, I shook my head.

"You must know," said Rauf, "the law looks unkindly on vagrants, beggars, and even simple wanderers."

I nodded.

"So that," added Rauf, "all people require protection."

"Even," Elena added, "when you look like innocence itself."

"But," Gerard proclaimed, while grinning and looking around as if to seek applause, "innocence is always the best mask!" He gave a sharp poke to Owen, who accepted it as before, in silence.

As I tried to grasp Gerard's meaning, Rauf called, "Your sister is in a convent. Tell us, do you think God is just?"

The question took me by surprise. "I . . . I want to believe so," I said.

"And that sister," asked Woodeth, "does she pray for you?"

"I . . . I hope so."

My reply made Gerard laugh. "He *is* young!" he hooted, which brought them to laughter that I didn't understand. I felt my cheeks grow hot.

"Shh now!" Elena scolded. "Well then, Master Crispin," she said, "to hear your story puts me to mind that God has willed it that we should take you in hand. *We* can care for you and set you to better use than you've been."

I dimly sensed other meanings lurking in her words. But in my weariness and gratitude, I could not untangle them.

When talk dwindled, we spread out on the ground for sleep. Rauf offered me a place near the fire's glowing coals.

"You'll be warmest here," he suggested.

Touched by his kindness, I lay down and took pleasure in the fire, which had settled into a few sputtering sparks. Yet, tired as I was, I could not sleep, my mind too engaged in my good fortune. What could be better than traveling with these English-speaking musicians toward a place from which I could go on? God had been kind after all.

The air grew colder. I could hear the others sleeping: Gerard uttering small grunts; Woodeth shifting restlessly, muttering and sighing; Rauf breathing deeply.

Comforted by the return of inner peace, I was just falling asleep when I felt a poke. I twisted around. It was the boy, Owen. He had crept close to me and was squatting down. In such light as there was, his thin face appeared gaunt, his large eyes full of fright. He kept darting looks over his shoulder.

"Yes?" I murmured, half asleep.

"You . . . you mustn't trust these people," he whispered.

"What?" I said, trying to make sense of his words.

"They're no good. Save yourself by running off."

I shoved myself up on an elbow. "What did you say?" But the boy, alarmed by my sudden movement, scurried away like a frightened rabbit.

Troubled, I sat up and looked to where he had gone and thought of his words—a clear warning. Only then, in the gloomy light, did I realize that the family had placed themselves in such a fashion as to surround me. Even if I had wished to go, it would have been difficult. Was that on purpose?

But . . . run off? I had no desire to leave. Why should I? These people had been kind to me. Welcomed me. Fed me. Why would I want to be alone again? I'd no reason to believe the boy. If anything, he seemed odd, perhaps a half-wit. And beyond all else, I was exhausted.

Angry with the boy for putting fright into my head, I lay back down and tried to squash such thoughts. But though I did not want to, I felt obliged to ask myself what knowledge I had of these people other than what they said? "Musicians." Yes, they had instruments. They played them. Allowed me join them in music and song. Moreover, Bear's kind of song. That meant much to me. And, I reminded myself, they fed me, welcomed me. As for their weapons, was it not a fair precaution in such a wild place?

I thought of what the woman said about Iceland, that it was far away and I would need a ship to get there. Though daunting, that was surely worth the knowing.

My thoughts returned to the boy. Who was he? They had not claimed him as one of their children. He didn't look like any of them. How did such a one come to be their servant? What made him speak to me that way? He seemed very frightened. Cowed. I had seen the men use him roughly. But to treat a child so was altogether common.

I tried to recall what I had been when younger. Was I like Owen? Frightened. Unwilling—unable—to speak? What was his tale? I decided I should try to learn more.

As I lay there, I felt another touch on my side. Thinking the boy had returned, I looked around. To my surprise, it was the monkey, Schim. He had slipped his leash. Bending close over my face, he stared intently at me, his small eyes sad and shadowy in the last light. I gazed back, examining his face, which seemed at once human yet not human, some droll mockery.

He climbed atop my chest, squatted there, reached out, and, with his tiny fingers, touched my nose, my lips, and my eyes. I let him. Midst his examination, Owen clicked his tongue softly a few times. The monkey scampered away, returning to where the boy lay, and crawled on his chest. Once there he appeared to fall asleep.

By then my weariness truly took hold. Convincing myself I had found good fortune, I began to drift off into sleep. Thoughts of fortune made me recollect a song that Bear used to sing:

> *Lady Fortune is friend and foe*
> *Of poor, she makes rich and rich poor also*
> *Turns misery to prosperity*
> *And wellness into woe*
> *So let no man trust this lady*
> *Who turns her wheel ever so!*

Despite the song, I told myself that my fortunes *had* turned for the better. With that thought, I propped myself up on my elbow and took one more look about. The boy was curled on the ground. There was just enough firelight left for me to realize he was staring at me, and his eyes were glistening with tears.

Wishing no part of his strangeness, I rolled away, gave thanks to the saints for sending me such kind people, and slept better than I had done in a long while.

10

N THE MORNING I opened my eyes to a dim dawn of cold ground mist that crowned the brown grass with brittle hoarfrost. Leafless trees looked as frigid as I felt. Higher still, a dull sun hid behind ashen-colored clouds. The whole world seemed gray.

The others were just awaking. They bestirred themselves slowly, not bothering with a fire. They yawned in sleepy awkwardness, scratched arms, pulled faces, and muttered more to themselves than others. Grumpy sleepiness meant almost no talk. They seemed like common folk, as ordinary as the clay with which Adam was first made.

I did attempt to look more keenly at these people by the light of the day, but saw nothing that might help me see them any deeper—surely nothing to prove Owen's words.

Under Elena's orders, the boy mutely doled out pieces of old bread in equal measures. As we stood eating, Schim suddenly leaped from Owen to my shoulder, reached down, and snatched the bread from my hand. I was too startled to do anything. Next moment he jumped back to the boy, where he quickly devoured it.

A scowling Rauf said, "Devil take him! He's the *best* thief among us!"

The others laughed, but the words *"best* thief*"* caught my ear.

Owen looked at me. At first I thought he was apologizing for the monkey's theft. Then I decided his eyes were pleading with me not to reveal his words of the night before. Having no reason to, I made a quick, tiny nod. His tension eased. I shifted away, only to notice that Elena had been watching me.

"Have you second thoughts about staying with us?" she asked.

The question took me by surprise. The very query— echoed by the boy's words of the night before—made me consider the choice of staying with them or going off on my own.

"May I leave?" I heard myself say.

If her question surprised me, my answer did the same for her. She studied me with a frowning face, lifted an eyebrow, and pulled back a step. Rauf had been walking away, but when he heard my words, he swung about and considered me with a scowl.

"When we talked last night," said Elena, "I thought we agreed that you would become our good companion. Did we not share our food and give you a fair welcome?"

All I could say was "You were surely kind, mistress."

Rauf drew closer by a step. "And if," he said, "we work together, Crispin, you must swear that we'll stay as one, at least until we're done with Calais."

Gerard drew closer, too. "To practice as six," he said, "and then perform as five seems unwise." Despite his toothy grin, he had his blade in his belt, and his hand was resting on it.

Woodeth, too, looked upon me, but her eyes seemed sad, and she said nothing. As for Owen, he stood very still, staring at me, mouth slightly open. He appeared frightened.

Ringed about as I was, I felt intimidated. How could I not be aware of the men's and Elena's rough irritability? Rauf's scowl showed nothing less than anger. Gerard's grin was belied by the hand upon his blade. The boy's words, "You mustn't trust these people," echoed in my head. I felt a strong desire to thank them for their hospitality and go my way. After all, Elena's words did not say I could not, or that they would keep me from leaving.

All the same, I was equally fearful of what might happen if I did go. Besides, I truly did not want to be alone. Those two things held me. I said, "If you'll have me, I'll join you."

"Good!" said Elena, her face softening.

I turned to Owen, wondering what he was thinking. If anything, his face showed sorrow. But from the others came a diminished tension and a gruff acknowledgment of welcome. Then they went about their business of getting ready to move on.

It was Woodeth who found a small cloak and placed it around my shoulders. I was grateful.

"Have you really heard of Iceland?" I asked her.

"By name only."

"You said it was beyond the sea. Nothing more?"

She shrugged. "Just what I told you."

All this left me uncertain of myself and them. I looked around for Owen. From the way he kept his eyes lowered, I sensed he was taking pains to avoid me. Instead, he busied himself by gathering things that lay about—cups, musical instruments, and boots—and gave them to whomever they belonged. The cooking things—two pots—he put into a sack, which he slung over his shoulder. The two men did nothing. I could see now how much the boy was their base servant. Nor did I hear any kind words bestowed upon him.

As I watched, I could not help seeing him as what I must have been—before Bear—and told myself that, whatever his weaknesses might be, I should be kind to him like Bear was to me.

Rauf, meanwhile, fixed his sword to his belt, while Gerard set a large blade on his hip. They carried their own instruments. I was given the recorder to carry. Owen had his sack. I offered to take it, but Rauf told me harshly it wasn't necessary. "The boy likes to be helpful."

The monkey took his place on Owen's shoulder and seemed determined to remain there. As for myself, I resolved not to worry, to think no ill of these people and be grateful for their company.

Gerard, in the lead, took a narrow path. Elena walked with Woodeth. Owen, monkey on his shoulder, sack upon his back, came alone.

Rauf took a place by my side. A cord around his neck

kept his bag close, while his bagpipe was slung under an arm. As he walked, he limped. The way he leaned over me made me uncomfortable, his bulk and broad shoulders making me feel small.

We went in a westerly direction and soon came upon a straight road with wagon ruts. With Gerard in the lead, we followed. I did not see a single dwelling. Happily the day edged toward greater warmth.

As we went along, Rauf kept me by his side. He did nothing to force me so. He simply stayed with me. Pleased to have me as a captive ear, he regaled me with more of his family's adventures, in Italian lands, the kingdom of Navarre, and Gascony. He told me of their performance in fairs, markets, the homes of rich merchants, and the fine dwellings of noblemen. Even castles.

"You'd be amazed at the fees and gifts they gave us," he bragged. "And you may be sure that if they tried to cheat us of our due, we found ways to balance the scales. Though I regret it now, that horrid monkey was such a taking."

"Why do you dislike him so?"

Rauf snorted. "He dislikes me."

"Why keep him then?"

"He came with the boy. And Owen's the only one who can get him to do tricks. You'll see: being a rarity, the beast draws crowds. He's a fine beggar."

"Where does the boy come from?"

He looked at me. "What makes you ask?" he snapped.

Taken aback by his sharpness, I said, "I was just curious."

Frowning, he said, "Best remember the saying: The curious guest ceases to be a guest." Then, as if to make amends for his brusqueness, he said, "He was a wretched begging boy. We took pity on him." He gestured toward Owen and grinned. "I admit, it's hard to know who's the smarter, boy or monkey. Still, we gained a servant. Two, in fact."

Then Rauf went on to boast of all he'd seen of the world, so much more than I. I confess, I marveled at the wealth, the wonders he had seen. Once again it felt good that I'd joined them. Perhaps their fortune would touch me.

"What happened to your recorder player?" I asked.

Rauf's mood shifted again. "You do ask questions," he said, frowning. Then, as if upon reflection, he said, "Master Mark? He joined us in Italy, only to decide he wanted nothing to do with us. It caused . . . a falling out. In Bordeaux." He touched a finger to his forehead scar. "He fared the worse."

In another of his ever-changing moods, Rauf abruptly shifted the fine bag that hung around his neck and held it open.

"Look inside," he insisted.

I hesitated.

"Go on," he said, thrusting it at me. "Look!"

I peered in and gasped. Even in the morning's dull light, I could see that it was filled with coins—silver and gold florins. I even saw a few gems, plus I knew not what other things of value.

"There is so much!" I exclaimed. It hardly fit their dress, or what I knew of their life. And what of Elena's words that they must earn their fare?

"We work hard for it," he said, grinning.

I recalled how much Bear and I made from our music: at best, pennies. That in turn made me recall the boy's words. I said, "And . . . and does all that come from your music making?"

He snorted. "Don't you know about Saint Jude?" he asked. "He of lost causes and desperate situations. I pray to him. You could do worse. Stay with us," he said, poking me on the shoulder, hard enough to hurt. "And we'll be far richer come Calais," he went on. "They say it's full of wealth. Sly lad, you picked the perfect time to join us."

He then set his bagpipe under his arm and piped some songs, telling me to play the recorder they had given me.

As we went on, making music, I again put aside my questions. Perhaps that was Rauf's intention. At the moment it did not matter. All I could do was walk on. But now I had two questions: Where did Owen come from? And in what manner had these people obtained such wealth? But I saw no way to get answers.

That morning we came near a small village. As soon as they spied it, we halted. Elena went ahead to purchase some food. Rauf barked some orders to Owen and then announced that he and Gerard were going to seek drink. Woodeth remained, as if to watch over the boy and me.

While she held Schim by his leash, Owen set about to gather some kindling from the edge of the woods. After a few moments—thinking Woodeth would not care, and eager to question the boy further—I began to work by his side.

"Tell me more about these people," I said under my breath as we picked up branches. "Why did you say I shouldn't trust them?"

Owen glanced furtively to see if Woodeth was watching. Without looking at me, his breath coming hard, he answered, "They . . . they warned me not to talk to you."

"Who did?"

"Rauf. Elena." He was finding it difficult to speak.

"Why?"

He went off a few steps to pick up wood. Then he

drifted back. "They don't want you to know what they are."

"What . . . are they?"

"Thieves. Murderers." His voice was shaking.

Startled, I looked at him.

"It's true," he whispered, making the sign of the cross over his heart.

"How . . . how do you come to be with them?"

His eyes filled with tears. His lips quivered. "They stole Schim and me."

"Stole?"

"From my older brother. After they killed him."

I could hardly believe what I was hearing. "But why? How?"

He went on in short, hurried bursts. "My father makes gloves. In London. Made some for the Duke of Sunderland. Then the duke went to Italy. My older brother, in the trade, traveled with him. So did I. I got Schim in Italy. Then the duke abandoned all. Since my brother played the recorder, Rauf asked us to join them as they traveled home. We learned they were thieves. When my brother didn't want to be a thief, they killed him. They told me they would take me back to my father, but I must be their servant."

I was truly speechless.

"They beat me," the boy went on, panting, lips quivering. "Treat me like a slave."

"Why don't you run off?"

"Where would I go? They say . . . they say they're going to take me to England. Return me to my father. For a price. I . . . every day I pray they will."

"Aren't they going to that city called Calais?" I asked.

He nodded.

I lowered my voice even further. "What do they want of me?"

He shook his head. "I don't know. It won't be good. Please!" he said urgently. "If Rauf learns I've talked to you, he'll beat me." He looked back around. "He beats Woodeth, too. I think her hurting makes her kinder to me."

With that, he moved away and attended to his wood collecting.

Greatly troubled, I stood in place. Then I turned. Woodeth was looking right at me. Even as I wondered if she had seen me converse with the boy, she beckoned me to her side.

I stood motionless, trying to make up my mind if I should just run off.

"Crispin!" she called.

I felt compelled to go. When I stood before her, she looked up.

"You need to know," she said, "that boy's head is weak." She touched her brow. "Full of folly. You'll do yourself no kindness listening to him."

Not knowing what to believe, I backed away, uneasy.

11

IN THE AFTERNOON, the skies were still gray and the air had remained cold. We were moving at an easy pace along the same road. Dense forest was on either side. Rauf was some ways ahead, followed by Elena and Woodeth, talking close. I wondered if Woodeth had told Elena of my talking to Owen. As for the boy, he was walking alone with the monkey, who, perched on his shoulder, chattered gibberish now and again. I very much wanted to speak to Owen some more, but took him at his word that I should not.

I came next in line. Behind all walked Gerard.

As we walked, I had a vague awareness that the family was surrounding me. No threatening words were said. Nothing done. It was the same as before: something I sensed. To push down such thoughts, I put my mind to Calais, hoping we would reach it quickly. Once there I would find an opportunity to go my own way and thereby rid myself of all these nagging worries.

I was just considering how I might seek more knowledge about Iceland and its whereabouts when I heard a sharp, shrill mouth whistle. I looked around. Before I could see anything, the whistle sounded again, three times in quick succession. Only then did I realize it came from Rauf, who had been in the lead. I had no idea how to respond. The effect on the others, however, was instantaneous.

Elena darted off the road and concealed herself behind some trees. Rauf dropped his bagpipe by the roadside, took his sword in hand, and darted into the woods as well. Woodeth ran to where I stood and grabbed my arm.

"Hurry!" she insisted. "Off the road." She fairly shoved me into the trees on the side. My cloak fell off. Owen and the monkey came with us. Within moments, the road was abandoned. I had no idea where Gerard had gone.

I assumed there was some danger ahead, which Rauf had seen, and that I was being hurried off for protection. Owen and Woodeth remained with me. Then I realized that Woodeth had a dagger in hand, which I had not seen in her possession before.

"What's happening?" I asked, quite bewildered. "Is there some danger? My cloak—"

"Be still!" she commanded.

Schim, alarmed, made rapid clicking sounds. Owen reached up and touched his face, which calmed him. But the boy looked at me with anxious eyes.

When I turned back toward the road, I saw a large wagon lumbering into view, its rear wheels bigger than the front ones. Pulled by a slow-moving ox, the wagon was loaded with bales and chests. Sitting high was an older man—I could see his white hair beneath a fur-trimmed Flanders cap. Seeing that his clothing was made of good cloth, I took him for a merchant with his goods.

A younger man, equally well dressed, walked beside the wagon. Even from a distance, I could see some resemblance. I took him for the merchant's son.

There was another man, an older, stooped fellow in russet peasant garb. He walked by the ox's head, guiding the beast with the light touch of a switch. Engaged in talk, the merchant and his son showed no awareness that we were close and watching.

Suddenly I saw Gerard, blade in hand, leap out from behind the trees. He took a stand in the middle of the road, blocking ox and wagon. Even as he did, Rauf appeared behind the wagon. The next moment Elena ran from her hiding place. In her hand was a short sword.

Gerard raised his weapon. "Halt!" he cried.

The peasant walking by the ox was taken completely by surprise. He grabbed the beast's yoke and hauled on it, bringing the wagon to a halt. The merchant put a hand to his mouth. His son, just as surprised, stood where he was.

"By your life," Gerard cried out. "Throw down your purse!"

All of this happened with such speed and design that I could have little doubt: these were practiced movements.

I turned toward Owen as if he might tell me something. But he was staring out at the road. I shifted back just in time to see the merchant's son—a sword in his hand—rush at Gerard.

Gerard, undaunted, backed up a few steps and engaged the young man with his own blade. I looked on, transfixed, while the clank and scrape of metal made me wince.

Then I saw Rauf approach from the rear of the wagon. He gave a shout. The young man, who appeared skilled with his sword, lunged and struck Gerard's arm. Gerard recoiled with a cry of pain. Even as he did, Rauf leaped forward and stabbed the merchant's son in the back. To my horror, I heard the young man cry out and saw him drop his weapon and fall as though mortally wounded.

The peasant, who had been standing by in shock, leaped away and fled into the woods. As for the merchant, who had remained on the wagon, he cried out and stood, hands lifted.

Elena rushed up to the wagon. "Get down!" she shouted, pointing her sword at him. Whether he understood English or not, her intent was clear. The old man all but fell from the wagon. But his eyes, I saw, were fixed upon the bleeding man on the ground. He tried to move toward him, only to have Rauf and Gerard block his way.

Elena dashed forward, yanked open the old man's gown, and stripped away a fat purse tied to his inner belt. Then Rauf pushed him roughly down upon his knees. The old man clutched his head and began to moan and cry piteously in French.

Rauf unhitched the ox from the wagon. Gerard, using the flat of his sword, smote the beast and sent him stiff tailed and bawling into the woods.

Next moment Elena climbed upon the wagon and made a hurried search. "Nothing but wool and cloth," she called before climbing down.

The merchant, meanwhile, remained on his knees,

weeping and gesturing to the injured man and crying, *"Mon fils! Mon fils!"*

Rauf responded by striking the man on the arm with his sword, bringing sharp screams of pain. "Be off with you!" he shouted into his face, and then kicked him. "Away! Go! Before we slay you too!"

The terrified old man staggered to his feet. Clutching his arm, he ran awkwardly into the woods, his fine robes flapping about him like a bird's broken wings.

As soon as he was gone, Elena and Rauf gathered around Gerard, concerned for *his* wound. After a quick look, Rauf stepped away and went to the murdered young man who lay upon the road.

That's when he turned and called, "Crispin! Come here!"

12

 WAS SO FRIGHTENED, I could hardly breathe.

"Go!" Woodeth shouted, and shoved me toward the road. I stepped out awkwardly. Rauf must have seen the fear on my face because he called out, "I'm not going to hurt you. Hurry!"

Gerard, looking on, held his wounded arm.

My legs trembling, afraid to look up, I went to where Rauf was. Elena and Gerard moved to stand over me, as if to overawe me.

Rauf gestured to the man on the ground. "See if he has a purse of his own." The poor man—his blood sinking into the earth—was no longer moving.

I stood there looking at Rauf. His face turned red with anger. "By the bowels of Christ!" he cried. "Do as I tell you! Find his purse!"

Upset and scared, I looked around. Gerard and Elena, breathing rapidly, stood there glaring at me.

With much self-loathing, I dropped to my knees by the body and with shaking hands felt about the dead man's bloody jerkin. His purse was tied to a belt. My fingers shook so it made untying the knot difficult.

"Faster!" shouted Rauf.

I struggled to strip the purse away, stood up, and, unwilling to look into Rauf's eyes, gave it to him. In haste, I wiped my bloody hand on my clothing.

"There," Rauf proclaimed as he took the purse, "Crispin has been baptized. He's one of us."

He reached out and twisted my face up, forcing me to look at him. He was grinning. Gerard threw back his head and laughed. Even Elena smiled.

"Quickly now," she commanded, grabbing my arm and hurrying me to where Woodeth and Owen stood. The boy looked at me with wide eyes.

"Stop gawking!" Rauf shouted at him and cuffed him on the side of his head. Putting up his hands, Owen staggered back. The monkey grimaced and hissed at Rauf. Rauf smacked the monkey, too, which caused him to shriek.

With Elena choosing the way, we all plunged into the forest. I stole a look back. The man Rauf had killed lay on the ground near the abandoned wagon, its wheels still. Even if I had tried, I could not have escaped. I was so terrified by what had happened, I did not make the effort. I had cast my lot with a band of murderous thieves, and they had forced me to be one with them.

Owen had spoken the truth.

13

WHILE ELENA'S FAMILY had no care for the young man they had killed or the old merchant they had cut and plundered, they had much concern for Gerard. Upon reaching a grove of closely gathered trees that Elena considered safe, they set him down, gave him ease and drink, and stripped his arm bare. It was soon apparent that though his wound ran blood, it was not deep. Woodeth attended him, and did so with care and skill.

As I watched, I couldn't help observing that amongst themselves they appeared loving, but to those left on the road, nothing.

Rauf, meanwhile, took himself and his sword and went some ways off to stand guard in case we were pursued. Within the clearing, I stayed to one side, and for the most part was ignored. All the while I kept trying to decide what

I should do. I must admit, my thoughts were not for those who had been brutally attacked. My great fear was that *I* might come to harm.

As I sat there, my eyes often went to Owen, who stayed with the monkey but apart from the others. Again and again the boy stole darting glances at me, only to turn hastily away as if fearful of being caught.

"It's not severe," Woodeth pronounced of Gerard's wound, and proceeded to bind his arm.

Relieved that he was in no danger, the family's mood eased. Elena fetched Rauf.

"Well then," he asked, "how did we fare?"

Elena, who had taken the merchant's purse, dumped its contents on the ground where Gerard could see it, as if to reward him for his pain. Into the pile she also flung the contents of the young man's purse, the one I'd been forced to take.

By their judgment, it proved to be a fair clutch of coins, the reckoning of which I could not begin to guess. They took great pleasure in examining the coins, debating where they had come from.

As they did so, a coin's glitter must have attracted Schim. Unexpectedly, the monkey leaped forward and plucked up a coin. Rauf was too quick for him. He smacked the creature with such force the beast was flung to one side. The coin fell from his grasp. Owen cried out as if he had been struck, but dared not move.

It took some moments before Schim got up, shaking his head as if dazed. As Rauf and Gerard laughed, the battered monkey scampered back to Owen, who gathered him up and wrapped his thin arms around him soothingly. The beast buried his head in the boy's neck.

"Since he's yours, keep him close!" Rauf shouted at Owen, scooping up the coin. He turned to me. "You'll see: the only thing he's good at is begging when we play. The moment he stops performing, I'll wring his neck. The same for the boy."

Rauf looked at the coin as if to determine its value and then pitched it at me. It landed at my feet.

"Take it," he called. "You've earned it. The beginning of your fortune."

I stared at the coin, confused and ashamed. With the eyes of all upon me, I hardly knew what to do.

"Pick it up!" shouted Rauf. "It's your fair wage! You've earned it!"

Silently praying to an understanding Jesus that He might forgive me, I took up the coin. By doing so, it was as if I had sealed the final part of a bargain. The Judas silver.

Indeed, as soon as I had the coin in my hand, they cried, "Well done! Bravo!"

I hung my head.

"Come now, Crispin," said Rauf, "did you not tell us you once killed a man."

"He . . . he set upon me," I admitted, not wishing to talk about it.

"Do you feel burdened by that death?"

"I do. And in Jesus's name, wish it hadn't happened."

"Would you say, then, that fate forced you to act?"

I squirmed with discomfort. "I . . . I was trying to save my father."

"The same with me and my good brother!" cried Rauf. "To save him, I had to kill that man."

I thought to say, but didn't: *But you needn't have attacked him.*

My silence seemed to goad them on. "Crispin," said Gerard, "as the bountiful Lord knows, we all call ourselves His good creatures. But are we not merely mangy dogs, forever fighting over scraps and bones?" He looked to Rauf, who grinned.

"Since God gave us life," Gerard went on, "is it not our obligation to live as best we may? Lords and kings are more successful at it. How do they do it? They tax the poor.

Well then, may not a poor man levy a tax as well? *They* have laws and soldiers to enforce *their* tax. We have our wits and blades. Is there a flea's breadth of difference?"

"A fair speech, brother!" cried Rauf, laughing.

How I wished I had words to answer him. When I said nothing, Elena said, "Crispin, I suspect you are young enough to be still trying to cling to your soul."

"I try," I murmured all too weakly.

"Mark me, Master Crispin," said Rauf mockingly. "In all of Christendom, there are but two sorts: thieves and those who supply the thieves with their needs. Each must choose which part to play. Did not Our Lord Jesus honor thieves when Saint Dismas—the good thief—was crucified with Him and joined Him in heaven?"

To my shame, I did not know how to answer. I caught Woodeth's eye. She was staring at me. I chose to see some sympathy. But she said nothing.

The money was all shoved into Rauf's bag—the one I had looked into before.

Their taunting done, I sat alone and brooded over what had been said. They seemed bent upon making me despise myself, seeking to make me like them. I told myself that a sinful life likes companionship just to ease the sin. I sought further consolation by choosing to believe they were only saying these things to salve their guilty souls.

As I sat there, I kept trying to imagine how Bear would have answered them. Or what Troth would have done. I eyed the bloodstains on my clothing. It gave me the thought: I had been privileged to be with Troth and Bear—whom I considered angels. Perhaps God had sent these devils to test me. Shuddering, I was sure that unless I could redeem myself, I was truly lost and damned.

The best I could do was put my mind to ponder what they might be planning for Calais. I began to fear that they had welcomed me to do some particular service. But what that might be, I could not imagine.

For the moment, however, Elena decided that Gerard should take his rest, which meant we traveled no more that day. During this time, I remained quiet, trying to be with them but not of them. No one told me I must remain. That said, many a furtive glance informed me I was being watched. My fear of them was such that I might as well have been in a dungeon. I had no doubt that if I had tried to escape, I would have been hauled back . . . or worse.

I watched Owen. He was ordered about by first one and then another of the family. He carried food. Cleaned boots. Beat dust from robes. Hauled wood for the fire and then tended it. While they talked among themselves—with little mind to him—not a word was shared with him, though both Rauf and Gerard occasionally administered a cuff or a kick. As the boy had claimed, he was treated like a slave. The only one who showed him any kindness was Woodeth, and that but an occasional soft word. Moreover, she did so furtively, clearly not wishing to be heard by the others.

When the day was done—we ate bread and cheese— and night closed in, they let me sleep where I chose. I kept telling myself I should leave. I didn't. It was not merely my fear of them. I'll not deny it: I found some safety in being with them. Better with than against. Besides, I kept telling myself that once they led me to Calais—which I doubted I could find on my own—I'd escape and find a ship bound for Iceland.

I settled down to sleep, as did the others. I don't know how much later it was when I was woken by a pull on my arm. I struggled out of my sleep to see Owen bending over me—as he had the night before.

"Crispin," he whispered very softly. "Are you awake?"

"Yes?"

"I've learned their plan."

I stared up at him and his poor, bruised face. "What is it?"

"They intend to steal from that merchant's house. The

place where they're going to play."

"I'm not surprised."

"You see how they treat me." He darted a look over his shoulder. "They'll do the same to you."

I gazed at him. "I'm going to leave them when we get to Calais."

He clutched my arm. "I beg you . . . take me with you!"

The request took me by surprise.

"Please," he whimpered, "I'll not live otherwise."

"If I can," I said, to his misery and without much thought.

"Will you . . . will you promise?"

I nodded.

He snatched my hand and kissed it, then retreated hastily into the dark.

I lay back, feeling alarm. Why had I made such a rash promise to the boy? How was I to help him when I could barely help myself? I should have held him off.

The very next moment I saw things in a different way, telling myself that here was a God-sent gift! If I could successfully aid this battered boy, I might go far in redeeming my soul by gaining some forgiveness for my part in plundering the dead man.

14

N THE MORNING Elena announced that Gerard was fit to travel. Besides, she reminded us, that wedding at which they wished to perform would take place soon. She was determined to reach Calais as quickly as possible.

Haste was fine with me. I could not get there—and then away from them—fast enough. As for Owen, he kept stealing glances at me in the most furtive of fashions. Fearful he would be noticed, I wanted to tell him to stop but dared not.

We set off, moving through the woods until we came upon a path, then a road, no doubt the same we had been on before. Once there I was in dread that they would find some new innocents and prey upon them as before. Happily, none appeared.

It was during the afternoon that I began to smell that mix of salt and seaweed which I remembered as being the sea.

"We're closer to the Calais border than I thought," Elena proclaimed with delight when we took a rest. "From here on we should have an easy time of it."

I saw Gerard and Rauf exchange a glance, but could make nothing of it. On the contrary, as we walked on, the musical instruments were brought out—Gerard excused because of his arm—and much merry music was practiced and songs sung. I played the recorder. It served to distract me from the chill. But once again I marveled at these people, able to play such sweet sounds and yet be so cruel.

The forest began to thin. The soil turned loamy. In places it became sandy. The sea smells grew in intensity. Then, just as we were coming around a clump of trees, where the land abruptly lay open, we saw soldiers.

Because we had come directly out of the woods, we saw them without their noticing us. Rauf, who had been in the lead, reacted swiftly and had us retreat in haste back among the trees. From there we were able to spy out with perfect safety.

I counted nine soldiers. All had metal bassinets on their heads and wore what looked to be leather jerkins over chain mail. Some were armed with swords; others held pikes. All of which meant they were in a state of warlike readiness. One of the soldiers—he had a white cross emblazoned on his chest—stood near a horse.

They appeared to be gathered around a fire from which a small curl of smoke drifted in the air. Moreover, their position suggested that they were encamped near the road upon which we were traveling. If we went forward, we would surely go near to where they were.

As we stared, no one spoke. I whispered, "Who are they?"

"Can't you tell?" said Elena, never taking her eyes from the soldiers. "The one near the horse is wearing the cross of Saint Denis."

"The sign of the French," said Woodeth.

"But . . . what are they doing?" I said.

"We must be close to the border," said Rauf. He spoke more to Elena than to me.

"The English pale should be just beyond," said Gerard.

"But we've not crossed the sea," I said.

"Fool!" said Rauf with his usual brusqueness. "I told you: Calais, though in France, is English. But the French control the outlying area to the east and south."

"What he means," Elena said to me more kindly, "is that these soldiers are blocking this road to keep anyone from passing into Calais."

"Is there war here?" I asked.

Woodeth pushed her hair away from her face as if to see better. "The French and the English are always at war."

"Let's pray," said Rauf, "there aren't more about. But may the devil take these." He spat on the ground.

Remembering what the French had done in Rye as well

as the awful consequences of our dealings with English soldiers, I asked, "Will they do us any harm?"

"Only if they catch us," said Gerard. "God's wounds, they have no love for the English."

As we stood there watching, Rauf kept glancing at me, enough to make me uncomfortable. Then, abruptly, he pointed some short distance away. "Crispin! Stand back there. Owen! You too!"

I looked to Elena.

"Do as you're told," she said.

Given no choice, Owen and I moved where we'd been told to go. The monkey, perched upon the boy's shoulder, chattered softly.

While Woodeth stayed near us, Gerard, Rauf, and Elena drew close and began to confer amongst themselves in low voices. I could not hear what they said. But more than once Rauf glanced in my direction. It made me uneasy.

After a while Elena turned. "Crispin!" she called. "Come here!"

Apprehensive, I went to them. As I approached, Rauf put a heavy arm around my shoulder and gathered me in while the others drew close. I felt small and trapped.

Rauf cupped my face in his rough hand and stared down at me. "We have a vital task for you," he said.

"What you're going to do," said Elena, "will be of great importance."

"And when you do it," said Gerard, "as you surely will, we shall feel very grateful toward you."

The mock camaraderie of their voices rankled in my ears.

Rauf—still holding me hard—glanced toward the French, then turned back to me. "There's no saying what those soldiers might do if we try to cross right before their eyes. Poor minstrels that we are, they might let us through."

"In God's world miracles do happen," said Gerard, "but then again, it might not come to pass."

"More than likely they would search us," said Rauf, offering me a knowing look.

My mind went to his money bag.

"So you must see, Crispin," Elena said to me, "it's not a chance we should take, is it?"

"I suppose not," I murmured, guessing that was what they wished me to say.

"You suppose correctly," said Rauf, grinning while giving me a rough shake. "You'll be pleased to know that when you first stepped out of the woods, I had the thought that you might be useful at such a place as this."

I could not tell if he was mocking me or not.

"What we need of you, Crispin," said Elena, "is to coax those Frenchmen away from where they are—away from us—so we can reach the city safely."

"Me?" I cried.

"Here's what you will do," Rauf said as if it were all decided. "We shall retreat back among the trees and then proceed that way." He gestured in an eastward direction. "As we do, you will go forth and attract the attention of those soldiers."

"But . . . how could I?" I said, shocked by what they were telling me to do.

"By walking that way," said Rauf, pointing in a westerly direction, toward some hills, "you'll attract them."

"Enough to bring them after you," said Gerard.

"And when you do lead them *there*," Rauf went on, "we, having gone east, shall cross northward over the plain. Of course, when you escape these Frenchmen, you can rejoin us."

"Together," continued Elena, "we shall make our way to the city."

"But . . . but," I said, finding it hard to breathe, "what if they catch me?"

"You'll need to make sure you don't let them," said Rauf with a false smile. "Because if they do—and Crispin,

I am nothing if not honest to you—they will most likely kill you."

I could hardly believe what they were telling me to do.

"But if you're quick," added Elena, "you'll live."

"Could . . . could Owen come with me?" I said, with perhaps too much hope in my voice.

"The boy?" said Rauf. He glanced around at Owen, who was standing with Woodeth. "Of course not. We need him. I realize he has become your friend. Fair enough. Just know, if you don't do what we ask, I promise you it will go the worse for him."

"What do you mean?" I cried.

An impatient Elena said, "Don't be stupid, Crispin. By doing what we ask, you'll keep the boy safe from harm. Is that clear enough?"

I could not reply. How could I? To protect themselves and their wealth, they were prepared to have me killed. And do harm to the boy. It took me some moments before I found tongue enough to say, "Will . . . will you . . . will you give me a weapon to defend myself?"

Rauf looked at Elena before saying, "We've none to spare."

"Crispin," said Elena, "if you're in danger, use your legs."

With a tumbling sense of dread, I glanced at Owen. He

returned my gaze. I don't know what message I was trying to send. I had hoped to save him, and now there was no great likelihood I could even save myself.

Rauf clapped a hard hand on my shoulder, swung me about, and walked me forcibly until I reached the edge of the grove where we had been concealed.

"Crispin," he said, as if confiding, "we wish you to be part of us. Consider this a test. The more you prove yourself, the more you'll be with us." He ruffled my hair in a gesture of affection.

Feeling only loathing for them all, particularly for him, I said nothing.

"Godspeed," said Rauf. With that, he gave me a hard shove, so that I fairly stumbled out of the trees and into open land.

15

ANDS BALLED INTO fists, struggling not to look back or burst into tears, I walked off a number of paces. Then I paused, took a deep breath, and tried to gain a full sense of where I was, how the land lay before me, and what I must do.

I was in an area where the forest had almost ceased to be, though here and about stood random trees and low stubble. These few trees were not tall and appeared to be windblown into grotesque forms, as if squeezed and shaped by some clumsy hand. As for the land, it was not entirely level but had scattered hills to the southwest, which rose to some height. To the east and north, it was flat and, to my eyes, lifeless.

The ground beneath my bare feet was softer than within the forest, damp and almost marshy. My toes could press into it. The air held a damp heaviness, ripe with the smell of sea. How far off the sea was I had no idea, but surely not so very far.

Overhead the sky was as gray and cold as dull battle armor, enough to make me shiver. Perhaps it was fear. For

I could see the French soldiers with perfect clarity, though they appeared not to have noticed me—not yet—for which I was grateful.

I glanced back. When I saw that the family had already gone, that I was abandoned, my heart seemed to squeeze with pain. I had to remind myself they had only done what Rauf said they'd do, move eastward through the trees while I went west.

Who, I asked myself, was my greater enemy: the family or the French? It was a sensation I had before: as if I were a kernel of wheat between two millstones, likely to be ground to powder.

For a few moments, I played with the notion that I might go directly to the French and tell them about Elena and her family in hopes they would provide a rescue. At least for Owen. I fingered the coin Rauf had given me, the one taken from the murdered merchant. Momentarily I considered bribing the soldiers. But I had little doubt it would not be enough.

Then I realized that since I could not speak their language, I could never even explain. In any case, being French, they might kill me before I could.

But then a new thought came to me: I was free of the family! I need not go back to their murderous ways. Next moment, however, I thought of Owen and my vow to rescue him. I'll not deny it: at that point I wished I had not given my word to help the boy. The next emotion I felt was shame that I should forsake him so. What if Bear—I chided myself—had acted that way toward me?

Tense, I glanced heavenward. How I wished I knew the names of all the holy saints Bear had called upon for each special need! The most I could whisper was "Heavenly saints, and you, dear Saint Giles, who have so blessed me with your favor, look over me!"

With a trembling hand, I made the sign of the cross. Commending my soul and my hope of heaven to my Maker, I turned, knowing it was time to attract the French soldiers' attention and lead them toward the west.

I decided, however, that if I drifted in a more northerly direction, I would also be going toward where I understood Calais was. That would mean there would be the forest on one side—the place from which I had emerged—and on the other, northern side, somewhere, Calais. Though it was to Calais I truly desired to go, if the need came, I might escape back into the forest.

With that plan in mind, I began to walk away from the soldiers, having little doubt that they would soon see me. That I was finally going at a steady pace served to calm me.

As I walked, I tried, by keeping my head down, to avoid looking at the French. My fright, however, had me constantly stealing glances to where they were. So it was that I had gone no more than a few hundred paces when I saw that one of the soldiers had shifted and was now facing in my direction. I began to walk faster.

It didn't take long before all the French soldiers were looking at me. Though I reminded myself this was only what I was supposed to do—lure them toward me—it was all I could do not to run for safety back among the trees. Trying to strengthen my will by staring straight ahead and whispering prayers, I kept on.

The soldier with the cross of Saint Denis on his chest climbed upon his horse and gestured to his companions. The whole French troop now began to move, not in any haste—I was, after all, a solitary boy. I supposed they were bored and had nothing better to do. But I could have little doubt they were coming after me. If so, I had been successful in my task. Simultaneously, as I grasped more than ever the risk into which I had been placed, my heart began to pound.

I glanced toward the forest, wondering if it was not better to seek safety. Then I looked in a southwest direction and considered the hills I'd noted before, wondering if I could reach the top. If I could safely reach it, I might have a better sense of how the land lay. Might even find some escape. Calais—my real goal—could be closer than I thought. I decided to try.

I walked faster, trying to act as if I were paying no mind to the soldiers. All the same, I kept glancing around. It served only to make the horseman begin to lope. His companions trotted by his side.

Though the French were still a considerable distance from me, fear took hold. I broke into a run, racing toward the hills. It was the worst thing I could have done. I heard shouts behind me. Glancing over my shoulder, I saw the mounted soldier coming faster after me. He was calling to me too, and though I did not understand, I could have little doubt he was telling me to stop.

Redoubling my speed, I reached the bottom of a hill. I clambered up, struggling, until, gasping for breath, I reached the high point. Once there I stood panting, heart beating to the point of pain.

Open, barren land stretched before me. But to the far north, I thought I spied something that looked like a walled city, with a few churchlike spires, which I assumed was Calais. I saw, too—or fancied I saw—a ribbon of gray upon the farthest horizon, which I took to be the sea. But between the place where I stood and that escape lay an expanse of emptiness. There was so far to go!

I also noted a multitude of small, meandering streams, many of which looked to be no more than ditches. Some had water in them, others not. There was even one right below where I stood. But though the land was broken in this fashion, I could not see any place to hide.

I looked back toward my pursuers. The one on horseback was coming directly toward me, moving at a steady pace. Those on foot were now moving between me and the forest. It took but an instant to grasp what they were doing: cutting off any retreat in that direction.

Undecided which way to go, I remained in place and stared at the dreary land before me, praying I'd find some way to save myself.

The soldier on horseback—now coming up the hill— began to shout. I had no understanding of his words, but saw only too clearly the sword he held aloft. Moreover, he had set his horse galloping toward me. I could have little doubt the Frenchman was intent on trampling me down, or at the least striking me with his weapon.

Terrified, I bolted down the far side of the hill.

Running as fast as I could, I all but tumbled down the hill. When I reached the bottom, I paused briefly, struggling for clear thought, trying to decide which way to go.

I glanced back. The horseman was now where I had been, atop the hill, looking down at me. Once again he cried out. Once again I ignored him.

I recalled there had been one of those streams before me. Unsure what protection it might afford—if any—but unable to think of anything else, I ran for it. In moments I reached its bank.

The stream was not very wide—no more than thirty feet—with a muddy, gently sloping bank and water flowing at a sluggish pace. Whether it was shallow or deep, I could not tell.

I looked back. In pursuit, the horseman was plunging down the hill.

I had no choice. I charged out to the edge of the stream only to sink deep into cloying, clinging mud that reached my knees. Worse, it held me. To go forward I had to yank up each leg one at a time. Every step took enormous effort and made a ghastly sucking sound. It was as if the mud were a greedy mouth, seeking to swallow me whole.

It took frantic efforts to move on, half stepping, half falling, forcing myself through mud and then into the stream itself. Once in water, I finally found sounder footing.

I was now able to walk forward, albeit clumsily. I dared not look back, but stumbled on with strained breath. The water quickly rose to my chest, the cold making me gasp. Then came new alarm: I didn't know how deep the stream might be, and I could not swim. Even as I kept going—I really had no choice— I feared that the water might rise above my head.

So it proved. As I pushed on, the river's bottom seemed to fall from my feet. In an instant I found myself floundering, sinking, and struggling for air. Certain I was about to drown, I kicked my legs wildly and thrashed my arms.

My blessed Saint Giles must have been with me. There proved just enough forward momentum to carry me on so that my toes touched firm bottom again.

The surge of relief I felt swept me on, enough so I staggered to the far side of the stream. There, as before, I had to work my way through thick mud until, at last, I crawled onto the other side.

Gulping for breath, spitting water, my shivering body coated with mud, I stopped and turned about. The French horseman had now reached the river's bank and was yelling at his horse, urging him forward. The horse, after some hesitation, went on, only to sink into the same morass of mud into which I had sunk. The horse, moreover, carried far greater weight than I and so sank deeper, completely hampering his movement. Snorting and whinnying, he thrashed wildly even while being sucked down.

The Frenchman grasped the danger. He flung himself off the horse and, while trying to avoid its frenzy, struggled to find his own footing on the more solid bank. Once he reached it, he stretched out for the horse's reins, grabbed them, and began to coax and pull the beast back to safety.

For the moment I was forgotten. I stood there staring until, with a start, I grasped that I was—at least for now—safe. Making the most of it, I turned and fled.

Though cold and wet, I ran as fast as I could, now and again looking back, relieved to see the Frenchman was still struggling with his horse. Surely he no longer cared about me. But then I wasn't looking where I was going, either. One moment I was running freely. The next moment I was hurtling through the air.

16

LANDED WITH a bruising thud that blew all breath from me. The plunge left me stunned, face pressed into the muddy ground. With my head spinning, I could not move for some time. At length I was able to roll onto my back and gaze up at the vast gray sky. All I could see was its emptiness.

Gradually I pushed myself up onto my knees and looked about. I had fallen into a wide, muddy ditch. It was not very deep, so I could prop myself up and peer over the bank to see if I was still being pursued. At first I could see no one. Only when I swiveled about did I see the French soldier. He was leading his horse away from me, his mount now appearing to be lame. With a deep breath of relief, I gave thanks to Saint Giles.

For a while I remained in place, wiping mud away from my face and arms until I felt more composed.

My sense of calm was only temporary. Though I had been safely delivered, my tattered rags were wet, I was cold, and the day was passing quickly. Shivering, I tried to think what next to do. Had Elena's family succeeded in traveling on to Calais? Was Owen safe? Which direction should I go?

I peeked over the ditch anew, wanting to be sure that the Frenchman was truly gone. He was. Even so, I feared to stand up, but took some time to study the land in all directions.

The ditch I had fallen into had a sharply cut bank and lay so perfectly straight I decided it had been made by men, not shaped by God. A small thread of water trickled down its center. It appeared to lead nowhere. Standing up, I tried to determine the best way to go.

When I had stood upon the hill, I had seen, in a northward direction, what I thought was Calais. Where I now stood, so low, I could no longer see it. But from the position of the sun, it was easy enough to determine which way lay north. Since the ditch I'd fallen into was cut along a north-south line, I chose to go in a northern way.

For some time I traveled in this fashion in hopes of seeing anything that might assure me I was going the right way. Wanting a better view, I climbed out of the ditch. Everywhere I looked, the land proved as desolate as it first appeared, made more barren by a chill twilight wind that had begun to blow. As it increased in force, it carried bits of sand, stinging my face and arms.

Looking around, not knowing what to do, I noticed what appeared to be the ruins of stone walls not too far away. I was reminded of the deserted village where I first met Bear, a place ravaged by the great mortality. Into my head even now came the song I'd heard him sing:

Ah, dear God, how can this be?
That all things wear and waste away!

When I considered the splintered timber that lay amid the widely scattered stones, I concluded that the buildings had been destroyed with violence—as if by war. Did not Elena say the French and English were always fighting here? No doubt, the inhabitants had been driven away or killed.

As the crescent moon rose above the eastern sky, I felt an increasingly sharp wind. With my clothing still damp, I was forced to contemplate a cold and lonely night without fire, food, or shelter. Moreover, I had no true idea how far away Calais was. It seemed best to seek some protection among the ruins.

It was dusk when I drew near the broken walls. The closer I came, the more wretched and wasted the rubble appeared. The cutting wind and daggerlike shadows shaped by moonlight made it appear like a shrine to war. It was a spot where Death himself might sleep.

I reached a wall no higher than my chest. It had been built of wood and wattle, but now seemed more likely to tumble and mingle with the debris about my feet. I made my way to the largest structure, another low and broken wall of stone, more intact than others. Between where it stood and a long mound of heaped-up stones was a shallow trench. Judging that the trench might afford some protection against the wind, I lay down in it. With cold skin against cold stone, I hugged my arms and gave myself over to a long and bitter night.

As I lay there unable to sleep, I began to think that—rough-hewn though it might be—I was already in my grave. When I wondered where Troth might be sleeping, a sob rose in my throat. Did she ever think of me? Did she regret having stayed behind? I pushed such painful thoughts away. Instead, I tried to convince myself that I would be safer on the morrow.

But as the moon rose higher and the wind began to sing a steady sigh, the cold increased. I began to wonder if I would last through the night. Was I about to die?

That made me think of Bear. It was easy to imagine his large shape, hear his booming voice, and feel his all-enveloping force. *Crispin*, I could almost hear him cry, *you young fool! God gave you life! Who are you to deny it? Be alive!*

His figure and voice were so vivid in my ear and inner sight, it made me whisper as if in prayer, "Dear Bear, forgive me. I herewith vow to live—in your and Jesus's names!"

Such thoughts of life and death made me think that the pile of rubble against which I was pressed might actually be a burial mound. It looked as if it could be. Just the thought was unsettling.

The more I thought the spot was a grave, the less I could *not* think on it. In the end I decided there was only one way to compose myself: push away some of the mound's stones and free my foolish head of such fretful fancies.

I swung up onto my knees and, by the light of the white moon, began to throw off stones. The hard work brought some heat within me. Once begun, I labored hard and continued as if in self-mockery. But that self-mockery turned piercing when, upon turning over a large last stone, I discovered a broken-jawed skull grinning up at me.

17

I STARTED BACK in fright. Moonlight revealed the skull to be old, brown, and smashed in on one side, as if the person had been struck and thereby killed. Perhaps he had been a man of importance. He might as well have been a nobody. What could he tell me, teach me, warn me about? Though it was empty of life, I felt the skull was observing me. Disturbed, I made the sign of the cross over it and murmured a prayer for the person's soul.

Even then I was not sure what to do. I had no desire to have a grinning skull for my night's companion. Yet the place I'd discovered was better than anywhere else I'd found. In the end I decided to stay where I was, but rebury the bones.

Again making the sign of the cross—this time for my own protection—I edged nearer to the skull. I was about to replace the stones when I realized that the skull was resting not on earth but on the edge of a box.

I peered closer—the eye sockets were staring right up at me—and realized the box was made of iron. I studied it, wondering if it might contain anything of value. The thought of pulling it out and opening it came to me. But though this was clearly not holy ground, I feared doing so would be disturbing a burial.

I went back to where I'd been and tried to settle myself. It wasn't long before the heat of my work left me. I became colder than before.

As I lay there, trying to control my shivering, I kept thinking about that box, wondering what it might contain.

Impulsively I scrambled around, knelt by the skull, and began to pull away more stones until the box was much exposed. When it proved larger than I'd first perceived, my fancy began to enlarge in equal measure. Perhaps it held gold, or jewels. I might be as rich as Rauf! I could buy my own and Owen's freedom.

I yanked away more stones until the box was completely uncovered. It was not so big that I could not wrap my arms around it. But to retrieve it, I would have to shift the skull.

Even as I told myself I might suffer for such actions, I gently shifted the skull—how weightless is an old death!— and pulled at the box. As I did, the skull fell back. In doing so, it twisted toward me, grinning, as if to watch what I was doing. Stifling my disquiet, I examined the box closely. Moonlight revealed a lid with a rusty clasp. I plucked it open and lifted the lid.

Inside was cloth. When I lifted it out, it proved to be a woven wool coat, enriched with some small embroidery as well as metal clasps. Beneath lay plain leggings, leather boots, even a dark over-tunic with a long-tailed hood. Nothing else. No purse or wealth of any kind. Yet to my eyes, what I had found was far better than jewels.

I gathered the clothing in my hands and felt its fullness and warmth. I did wonder why the clothing had been left. Perhaps it was all this man had, his only wealth. Or possibly he'd been wrapped in a shroud, and these things were set aside in due respect.

Should I take them? I recalled what Bear—in my thoughts—had said: "God gave you life! Who are you to deny it?" Had I not believed it a sin to take money from that man Rauf murdered? But then there were Gerard's words, that we're "merely mangy dogs, forever fighting over scraps and bones."

Was that what I was: a mangy dog, about to steal some scraps of warmth?

Gazing at the dead man's bones, I told myself that this man's soul was—praise God—somewhere sweet, that he had no use for such garb. Not as much as I.

I decided to believe Bear had answered my prayers by bringing me these remains. With that reassuring thought,

I pulled off the tatters I had worn so long—with their foul, bloody stains—and replaced them with the dead man's clothing: leggings, jacket, hood, boots, and finally, the over-tunic. They were large for me, but not by very much. Beyond all else, they warmed me wonderfully well. In all my life, I had never been so clothed!

As I changed my garments, the coin that Rauf had given me clinked to the ground. Briefly I considered leaving it as an offering, but told myself I might have a need.

Closing the box with a clank, I returned it to where it had been, replacing the skull where it had rested on the box's edge. With care, I put the stones back as well.

Once again I whispered prayers for the dead man's soul, adding words of gratitude and thanks. That done, I went back to my place and gathered my new clothing about me, the hood pulled around my head. With such kindness as the angels had bestowed upon me, I was certain I would survive for the night. I'd be able to find Owen.

That gave me another thought. In helping Owen, I would be acting as Bear had done for me. The thought that I was like Bear—if only to a small degree—caused me to grin and filled me with satisfaction.

And so I slept—kept alive by one dead man's clothing and another's acts of love.

18

HOUGH MORNING SUNLIGHT coming over the broken walls opened my eyes, the warmth of my new garments kept me drowsy. In all my life, I'd never woken to such woolly softness. Rare luxury!

For a while I was content to lie in my newfound ease, breathing cold air seasoned with the scent of sea. In the sky overhead, raucous birds whirled about as if I was an intruder in this empty place. No doubt I was.

Stretching, I turned somewhat, only to come against some stones. They brought me back hard to where I was and the peril I was in: alone in an unknown land, and now very hungry.

Reminding myself that I must go on and find Calais and Owen, I murmured one more prayer for the soul of the dead man from whom I'd taken the clothing, begging forgiveness. I also made a prayer of thanks for my survival and took the time to beg a blessing for the unfolding day. That done, I came to my feet and adjusted my new cloth-ing. Only then did I survey the land about me in the clear light. Thankfully there were no soldiers. All I saw was barren emptiness: an open, marshy land with an occasional dune on firmer ground. Recalling that my way lay north, and using the sun as my guide, I set off.

At first I simply trudged along, constantly looking for people or something to eat. The land beneath my feet remained soft, often sandy, with countless streams and rivulets. There were brooks and water ditches that I had to wade across, holding my new boots over my head. I passed more ruins, too, some that seemed like decayed fortifications, as well as the remnants of small dwellings. I saw no people. All was forsaken, abandoned. And there was nothing I might eat.

Trees were rare. The little vegetation that grew was sparse and low. I wondered if Troth could have made anything of it. But as I passed a tuft of grass, a startled bird flew up. I searched and uncovered a nest with two small, speckled eggs. I broke them open and poured the contents into my dirty hand. One yellow yolk had a streak of blood. Though I considered it an ill omen, I swallowed it all down.

As I walked along, I gradually saw before me what I assumed was the crown of Calais: two church spires. As I would afterward learn, one was dedicated to Saint Mary, the other to Saint Nicholas, he who protected sailors.

Drawing closer, I saw the tops of other tall structures,

including a building big enough to be a watchtower. Then I spied a wide spread of stone wall that ran east to west. I was reminded of Great Wexley, the city where I had been with Bear, which was surrounded by circular walls. Here, however, the walls were long, straight, and high, built of large stones. Square towers were placed at regular intervals along the wall, round ones at the corners.

Drawing closer, I discovered that the city had double moats protecting its southern side. The first was right below the walls. The second was separated from the first by a mound of earth. The moats—with their filthy water— forced me to walk toward the east.

As I went along, armed soldiers spied down at me from the city walls. Wearing helmets, they were armed with pikes and crossbows. Though they did not look so very different from the French I had encountered, I assumed they were English.

I began to see ordinary people. For the most part, they were traveling alone, and of the few groups, none was as large as Elena's family. Among them were two heavy wagons pulled by horses. All were proceeding in a line, as if upon a road. I could have little doubt: this was the way into Calais.

It took a short time to reach the road. It proved to be

a roadway somewhat elevated above the marshy land. For the most part, the people on it appeared to be merchants or peasants coming from the northeast. I looked to see if any of the wagons was the one the family had plundered. Happily I didn't see it.

When the road veered around the eastern wall, I discovered that the depth of the town was far less than its width. But while I could see that Calais was not a very large town, the number of building tops and high towers suggested a crowded place. The largest tower I'd seen from a distance now displayed a flag with a red cross.

As I hurried along, I heard bells ring, slow and steady. From the sun's placement in the sky, I guessed it was the hour of prime, and the bells were calling citizens to early mass. Once again my thoughts went to Troth. Was she at the convent church? Was she treating someone's ailment, or gathering herbs in the woods? How different—and quickly—had our worlds become!

A little farther on, I spied the sea, or rather a bay that led to the sea. The tide was low, the smell of fish and seaweed strong. In the middle of the bay was a small island on which stood a fortress commanding the sea entry. More importantly, I noted many ships. Some were coming in or leaving the bay. Some were tied to wharfs or hauled up on the shingle. One large ship was a hulk. Some of the larger boats I recognized as cogs, the kind of ship in which Bear, Troth, and I had come to France. I had no love of that memory. One cog, its single reddish brown square sail flapping idly in the light breeze, was being pulled to sea by a high-prowed long boat with men at oars. For the most part, though, what I saw were a slew of small fishing craft: crayers, pikers, and ketches.

I wondered if all had come from or were going to England. Please God, I thought, just one for Iceland! The thought excited me.

Despite the early hour, the scene before me was extremely busy. The dock area consisted of two wharfs, plus other landing places for the loading and unloading of ships, complete with ropes and lifting spars. Mariners and laborers were struggling with sacks, bales, chests, and barrels. Other men were working on the ships, replacing old rigging, cleaning, or making repairs. There was a steady rap of hammers. Midst it all I saw what I took to be merchants in fur-trimmed over-tunics and fine Flanders hats. In more than one hand, I saw an abacus. Armed soldiers were strolling about, too, as if keeping watch. There were even men whose flowing capes and looks of self-importance pronounced them officials of some sort.

I'll not deny it: it came to mind that I should just go among these boats and find—if I could—a ship bound for Iceland. How easy to board it and be gone! Elena's family would never know. But to think of the family was to think of Owen. My promise to Owen tugged at me. The constant thought—if I was to be like Bear, I must act like him—turned me toward the city gates.

As I went forward, I noticed a gallows at the far western side of the dock area. It gave me pause, the more so when I saw a body dangling. Swinging in the wind, it was black with rot, its stench putrid. It made me recall the ghastly corpse I'd come upon when I first fled my village. In haste, I made the sign of the cross, averted my eyes, and moved toward the city gates.

Even so, I could not help but look back at the gallows and its victim. It made me wonder if I were about to pass through the gates of hell.

19

UILT INTO THE WALLS, the entry to Calais consisted of a massive stone struc-ture with a huge front gate of thick iron bars, which could be lifted and dropped by ropes. Poking out from these walls at an angle was a watchtower that looked down upon the entryway. Along its crenellated top, soldiers stood on guard.

Before the gate was an area paved with small stones. It was there that soldiers were questioning people seeking entry to Calais. Indeed, the city—with its walls, moats, tow-ers, and soldiers—seemed a hard knot of war and defense, exceedingly difficult to enter.

Since the soldiers were closely examining everyone, the throng moved slowly. The one who appeared to be in charge was a soldier. A captain, I supposed. He was a tall, florid-faced man with a loud barking voice. His boots were high, his hands gloved. At his hip was a heavy sword. It would have taken a brave man to challenge him.

As I edged closer, I tried to learn what was being asked, wanting to be prepared with acceptable answers. It turned out the captain was demanding to know where people had come from—what ship or town—and what manner of business they might have in Calais. Other soldiers were searching through baskets, poking into bales, and opening chests.

"Are they looking for something?" I asked a mariner who stood in the line before me.

"Smuggled goods."

"Is it hard to gain entry?"

He made a grimace. "Just as hard to get out."

"Why?"

"They will tax whatever goods are brought in or out." He spat upon the ground.

For the most part, the people wishing entry were mariners and claimed—usually speaking English—that they had come off one ship or another and needed to reach masters already at the markets. Some of the people passing through spoke French. There were peasants, too, with baskets of food to sell. The captain reminded all that the city gates closed when the night bells rang for compline and would not open again until prime. No exceptions would be made.

"Boy! Step forward!" came the cry when it was my turn. I took a deep breath, told myself not to be fearful, and walked forward.

The captain looked down at me with hostile eyes.

"Quickly, boy! What brings you here?"

"Please, sir, I was with a group of musicians hoping to play at the wedding feast that will be given by Master Humfrey Talbot for his daughter."

"Why aren't you with them?" he demanded.

"We became separated," I replied with a measure of truth. "Have they passed through?"

"I've no idea. A fair number of musicians have arrived," he allowed.

"A family of five?" I said.

"I can't say," he returned gruffly. "All right. Pass along! Hurry!"

Much relieved, I hastened forward and finally entered the city of Calais.

After being in the open for so long, I was overwhelmed by the swarming city. The people were like penned sheep, a mass of men, women, children as well as horses and oxen. Citizens were generally of the poorer sort, but I could see numbers who were wealthy. They were all clothed in brown or black, with an occasional priest in white. Here and there a rich person arrayed in brilliantly colored cloth passed by, leading well-dressed servants.

The streets were stone paved while the closely built houses were timber framed, plastered with white or yellow-brown clay. These houses were generally two stories high, although a few buildings had a third level hanging over the street. Many buildings bore flags and banners, as well as signs proclaiming the goods sold within, such as bread, tools, shoes, or cloth. Crowds of people were buying and selling, crying, "Hot pies, hot!" "Wine of Gascony!" "Flanders caps!" "Fresh water!" Armed soldiers strutted about like big, plump geese, and people made way for them. Over all was an intense city stench—dung, rot, bread, ale, and sweat.

Great Wexley's streets had gone all which ways. In Calais, however, they ran in straight lines. Even so, when I first entered and began to wander, I kept coming upon the outer walls. Once I came upon a corner where walls joined. A round tower was set there, its entryway open, revealing stone steps that led to the ramparts.

At length I crossed over two narrow streets and stepped into a huge market area, far longer than it was wide, dominated by a tall central tower. At the far end of the market was a huge and bulky fortress.

The main market was crowded with stalls, tents, and pavilions of all sizes. Here was selling of a different order than on the streets: huge bales of sheep's wool were everywhere, some open, some tightly wrapped with cord.

Merchants and tradesmen were bargaining in loud voices. I saw many coins exchanged and heard the clicking abacuses as accounts were reckoned. For the most part, English was being spoken. But I heard French, as well as other tongues unknown to me.

While the wool market was a major part of the trade, there was another large section in which quantities of fish were being sold. Some was fresh, but much was salted away in barrels. Then there were other parts where quantities of food, pottery, baskets, and clothing were offered.

I had never seen such a crowded place, not even Great Wexley. The throng was so thick, I hardly knew where to turn. Even so, I kept searching—often having to push my way through—constantly looking for members of Elena's family.

Then, above the clamor, cries, and shouts, I recognized that skirling bagpipe sound. I had little doubt it was Rauf and the family. How different it sounded to me now! I hated these people. How then to explain the joy and relief I felt? It took me by surprise.

I followed the sound, and sure enough I spied them—encircled by a crowd—playing their instruments. Elena stood before the others, singing. Gerard had his harp, Rauf the bagpipe, Woodeth her mandola. Owen beat his drum.

In front of all was the monkey, Schim. Holding Rauf's red cap in his paws, he approached people, begging and receiving coins.

Owen saw me first. The moment he did, he smiled broadly, only the second time I'd seen him do so. Then the other members of the family caught sight of me. They seemed startled that I was there, exchanging vexed looks. Nonetheless, it took only a moment before they shifted their response and acted welcoming—without ceasing their music making—with smiles and nods of greeting, which I had every reason to distrust.

Rauf even paused in his playing to rummage in his sack, which lay at his feet. From it he pulled up the old recorder and held it out. I took it and joined in the performance.

I do not know how long we played—not so very long—but at length the crowd's interest waned enough that Elena called upon us to stop. When we did, Rauf snatched his cap from Schim—who hissed at him—took out the coins, and put them in his bag. Once released, the monkey darted to Owen, leaped up, and perched on his shoulder.

Meanwhile the whole family gathered around me with a cascade of questions:

"When did you arrive?"

"By what route did you come?"

"How did you escape the French?"

"How did you get here so quickly?"

"Where did you get your new clothing?"

I related what I had done, which they received with approval, even laughter. Indeed, they acted as if they were truly glad that I had rejoined them. In particular, they were much amused by my account of how I came to have a new set of clothing.

"Ah Crispin," cried Rauf with a clap upon my shoulder, "that's twice you've stolen from a dead man. You're a true thief."

Elena threw him a look of irritation, but to me she said, "Just know we're glad to see you."

My eyes went to Owen, who stood beyond the others. He made a small shake of his head.

I understood him all too well.

20

T HE FAMILY HAD arrived shortly before I did and had yet to find the house where the wedding was to occur. Though Elena decided it was time to find Master Talbot's home, they did something I found curious. Rather than dip into Rauf's money sack, they used the pennies they had just earned with their playing to buy some bread. I took it that was meant to show how very little they had.

We left the market area and, with instruments in hand, returned to the narrow streets, where Elena asked directions. It fell out that Master Talbot was a major merchant in the wool trade and was well-known. We were soon directed to a Purfleet Street.

As we went along, Gerard made a point of staying close to me, insisting I hear how *they* came to the city. It was of such little account, I grew suspicious of his chatter. Stealing a glance back, I saw Elena and Rauf in intense conversation. The moment they saw me looking at them, they broke off. I had little doubt they were talking about me and that my returning to them had upset their plans.

It was not long before we stood outside Master Talbot's

house. It proved to be a large timbered structure of three levels. Its sheer size proclaimed it the home of a wealthy man. Bright-colored flags flew from poles. Banners draped from many windows, windows that even had some glass.

On one side was an entryway, which appeared to lead to some place of business where merchants were coming and going. On the other side was a door to the house itself, guarded by two men in bright yellow and red capes. One of the men was older than the other. He was a portly, sallow-faced fellow with a girdle of keys about his ample waist that suggested he was the steward. He smelled of some sweet perfume. Elena approached him.

"Worthy master," she addressed him after making a deep bow. "We've come far to bring music to Master Talbot's daughter's wedding."

"You've arrived in good time," the steward returned. He was eyeing the monkey suspiciously. "What's that beast?"

"A performing monkey." Elena beckoned to Owen, who set Schim on the ground and bid him jump. He did a somersault.

Despite the steward's gravity, he grinned. "That will amuse the bride. Let's hear your music skill."

"Quickly, now," said Elena to us, "do your best!"

We lined up and began to play, but after a few moments,

the steward waved his hand. "Enough! Well done. My master will be pleased. Enter. Just make sure you keep that beast on his tether."

It was the other, younger servant who led us into an enclosed courtyard, where there were many people milling about. Most appeared to be cooks, bakers, and vintners bringing food, preparing for the wedding feasts. In one corner were other musicians with their instruments, practicing. They gave us a nod, which Elena returned, even as we were led on.

The servant took us to the back of the building, into a large hall with an arched ceiling. The hall was lighted by many candles, the air perfumed. A central fireplace glowed with warmth.

There were tapestries on some walls, white plaster on others. In the middle of the room, long trestle tables had been set up, though I saw no benches. The floor was strewn with sweet green rushes.

"You'll perform up there," the servant said, pointing to a balcony, which overlooked the hall. It was opposite a raised table at the other end of the room. "Master Throckmorton, the steward—with whom you just spoke—will inform you of your time."

We were led behind the building, passing through a

crowded, bustling kitchen, to a place where a series of sheds and stables stood.

"You'll stay here," the servant informed us.

Our shelter was a horse stable, each stall having three sides of rough wood wall, large enough for two horses. Overhead was a solid roof and deep, fresh straw on the ground where we could sleep in some comfort.

"The cesspit is around the back," the servant told us. "When supper is available, you'll be called. Be advised: there is much work to be done, so my master may require your assistance."

Rauf frowned and exchanged a knowing look with Elena. He gestured to me. "You may call on that boy."

The servant marked me with a look, nodded, and left.

"These rich people think they buy us whole," said Gerard with disgust.

"We'll do well enough," Elena assured him.

Woodeth looked the stall over. "We've slept in worse," she pronounced.

To which Rauf, in a low voice, added, "It will be made up in payment. There are great riches here."

They laughed.

After setting their belongings down, Rauf announced that he and Gerard would seek a tavern. For her part, Elena said she would return to the kitchen to find some food. She told Woodeth to remain with Owen and me.

"They can take care of themselves," Woodeth protested.

"Do as you're told!" Rauf commanded as he left.

The three went off. Woodeth, clearly peeved, glared at me. "Well, Master Crispin," she said, "your return has upset their plans."

"Why?" I said, truly confused. "How do you mean?"

She shook her head. "Do you think they would tell me? If you want my advice, be on your watch. Especially with Rauf."

She would—or could—say no more, but sat herself down against the stable wall, all the while keeping one arm protectively around Rauf's sack. As if to withdraw from the world, she closed her eyes.

For a brief time, I considered grabbing Owen and bolting away. I doubted, however, that Woodeth was truly asleep. Even more, I feared Elena's sudden return.

Beckoning, I got Owen to retreat into the far back of the stable, where we sat side by side. Schim stayed in the boy's lap.

"You see," I whispered to him, "I didn't forget you."

His grubby fingers clutched my hand, as if wanting to

be sure I was there and that I would not leave him. "They were sure the French would catch you," he said, his low, shaky voice revealing his emotions. "That we wouldn't see you again. You heard what Woodeth said. That's what they wanted."

"But why?"

"They don't trust you."

He looked over to Woodeth to see if she was listening. Satisfied she wasn't, he drew closer.

"Because I don't speak much," he said in a small, breathy voice, "they don't think I listen. As soon as you left, they talked as if I weren't there."

"What did they say?"

"That it would be good if the French took you."

Upset, I just looked at him.

"They feared you wouldn't obey them," he explained. "Elena called you a pious priest."

I nodded toward Woodeth. "What was she warning me about?"

He shook his head. "I don't think she knows. They don't tell her things."

"Can you guess?"

He glanced up at me. "Some other way to use and get rid of you."

"Why don't they just tell me to go?"

"They fear what you know of them. Is it true Rauf showed you their money?"

I nodded.

"They spoke of it. Elena berated him." The boy fingered my new cloak. "Did you really find your clothing on a dead man?"

I nodded. "I was cold and wet. Then you know nothing of their plans?" I pressed.

"Just that they intend to steal from this house."

"We'll get away first," I assured him—and myself.

"Will you . . . will you really take me with you?" He stroked the monkey's back. "And Schim?"

I nodded. "To Iceland."

"Is that far from England?"

"I'm not sure," I admitted. "We'll need a ship. But there are many here. And—God grant it—we'll find one bound the proper way."

"Will . . . that be hard?"

"I'll find a way," I said, wishing I truly knew.

"I . . . I don't care where I go," he confided. "I'd rather die than stay. But—"

Elena returned.

As Woodeth bestirred herself, I wondered if she had

heard anything of my talk with Owen. I reminded myself that I must be careful. In truth, I could have little doubt Owen was right: these people would find some way to use me for ill. That gave me but one task: we must get ourselves away as soon as possible.

21

ELENA BROUGHT BACK barley bread and new cheese, which, quite famished, I ate readily enough. Owen ate too, sharing some of his food with Schim.

"It's all that Rauf had hoped," Elena announced gleefully. "There's fine goods and money here. And the food: you should see how much! Boar's head, venison, swan. Lark pies and tarts. Spiced wines. Eggs aplenty. No end to it! A great wedding feast.

"And Crispin," Elena went on, but in a lower voice, "you'll be pleased to know that someone in the kitchen whispered to me that Master Talbot is not just a merchant, but a smuggler. You see, we're no different than the rest of the world."

Not wishing to talk about that, I said, "When will the wedding happen?"

"In two days' time," Elena replied with real excitement. "With festivities to last three days. The master's daughter is to marry a rich merchant from Bruges. The musicians come from many places: England, Hainault, and Flanders."

"With all the ships here," said Woodeth, "we should have no trouble getting to England." The way she looked at me made me wonder if she had heard my words with Owen.

Elena said, "Crispin, are you coming with us or going to that Iceland you spoke of?"

"To England," I lied, "surely."

"Then you can come with us," said Elena.

The truth was, I had no reason to believe any of them. Not after what they had done. Not after what Owen said. But now that I had returned, they seemed to want to make sure I remained with them. I suspected they already had made a plan what to do with me and did not wish me to slip from their grasp. But I could only guess at what they intended.

For a while no one spoke. I sat there, frustrated, trying to consider what I should do. My best notion was going to the market. My hope was that in such a busy, crowded place—with so many seafaring travelers—someone might tell me how to find Iceland.

As I sat there, keeping my hand warm in my inner pocket, I fingered the coin Rauf had given me. I glanced at Owen, who was shivering in his ragged tunic. It gave me an idea. "If this wedding feast is so fine," I said to Elena, "I'd like to get some better clothing for Owen." I held up the coin.

A startled Owen turned around even as Elena and Woodeth exchanged looks of indecision.

After a moment Elena said, "It's always better to appear well at these feasts. And you're almost elegant in your dead man's clothes," she added with some mockery. "If you wish to waste your money, I suppose Owen could look better."

Woodeth, clearly eager to get away from the stable, said, "There are many shops. I'll go with them."

Though that disappointed me, I said nothing.

"But let the monkey stay with me," said Elena with a smile I took to be false. "Then I'll know you'll come back."

After a moment's pause, Owen gave up the beast. Elena wrapped the leash about her wrist and gave a harsh tug. Schim had to stay.

The three of us set off.

We did not go through the house but along the narrow

alley that lay behind, then on to a regular street. The church bells had already struck sext, but when we reached the market, it was as crowded as the morning.

What I needed was a ship for Iceland. Of course, I would not find one in the markets, but my hope was to find someone who could offer some help. I kept trying to think what Bear would advise. Beyond being patient, I could think of nothing and had to be content to walk a step behind Owen and Woodeth, who meandered along in no great haste.

At length we came upon a shop over whose door hung a sign that bore an image of a sheep. A woman was standing by the door, trying to draw in buyers. She wore a headband, with two long braids hanging down over her chest. The plain brown kirtle she wore was ankle-length, with long sleeves. It looked newly made.

Woodeth pushed Owen forward. "Mistress," she announced to the shopkeeper, "this boy needs a simple garment."

The woman swept disdainful eyes over the excited Owen. "Be so good as to enter."

We stepped into a small room crowded with two low tables. Such light as there was came from three tallow candles on sticks. On one table lay folded cloth. Behind the other a man sat sewing. In a corner another man sat at a loom, weaving. When the woman began to show off her goods, I decided to take a chance.

"It's too crowded here for me," I announced, giving my coin to Owen and retreating before Woodeth could object.

Once outside the shop, I leaned against the doorframe and observed the crowd going by. There were plenty of peddlers and hawkers, offering all kinds of wares. "Pins!" cried one. "Pieces of horn!" cried another. And then I heard it: "Stockfish from Iceland!"

22

I T TOOK A MOMENT for me to grasp what I had heard. By then the seller—a boy—had already passed by. I bolted after him and caught him by an arm.

"What do you want?" he cried, twisting away with much annoyance.

"Are your fish truly from Iceland?" I asked, breathless.

"Of course they are. Dried to perfection," he said. "Six

for a penny." He held one up. It was twice as large as my hand, dull gray in color with dry, sunken eyes.

"But . . . where do they come from?"

"Are you deaf? *Iceland!*"

"In faith," I said with growing excitement. "Do you know where that is?"

"Not I."

"Then how do you come by these fish?"

"A man in the market"—he pointed—"offered me a penny if I would walk about and sell."

"What kind of man?"

"You are a dunce! A fisherman. With a white beard. Do you wish to buy or not?"

I could barely contain myself. "Did he come from Iceland?"

"How should I know? Leave me be," said the boy, and he went on, crying, "Stockfish from Iceland! Stockfish from Iceland!"

I looked back, prepared to follow, only to see Owen step out from the shop wearing a new kirtle. It was woolen, plain gray in color, and reached his bare feet. Long sleeves were folded back at his thin wrists. It was far too big. But his face, showing great—and unusual—pleasure, offered me a look of gratitude as he returned the few coins that remained.

Woodeth also emerged. "We'd best go back," she told us. "Rauf will be annoyed."

Owen and I walked side by side. He kept fingering the cloth of his new garment. "Thank you for your gift," he whispered. "I've . . . I've never had so fine."

"I've a better gift," I said under my breath.

He looked up at me.

In a small voice, I said, "I may have found a ship from Iceland."

First his eyes grew wide, but the next moment he slapped a hand over his mouth to hide a grin.

As we approached the stable in which we had been quartered, I heard Gerard say, ". . . Rauf will arrange. With as little pay as these soldiers receive, they'll be happy to gain more. All we need do—"

The moment we appeared, he stopped talking.

He and Elena were sitting side by side on the straw, against a side wall. Rauf was sprawled out, asleep, the stink of ale about him.

As soon as Schim saw Owen, the monkey started to chatter, broke from Elena, and leaped on the boy's shoulder. When Owen gave him a stroke, the beast quieted down.

Elena considered Owen's new clothing.

"Well done," she said. "A true improvement!" She stood

up. "Crispin, come! I need to introduce you," she said to me, glancing back toward Gerard as if he understood what she was doing. Though mystified, I went with her.

By then all the stable stalls were filled with musicians, some of whom spoke English, others not. Elena introduced me to many. Though these people did not seem to be very interested in meeting me, she made sure I was noted.

These musicians had many instruments, some I'd never seen before. Elena gave them names: a metal trumpet, a psaltery with strings, a bowed fiddle, a lute, even something she called a hurdy-gurdy with a turning wheel.

Elena was still making her introductions when the steward, Master Throckmorton, appeared. He called for all the musicians to stand before him—and that included Rauf, Gerard, Woodeth, and Owen. When they had gathered in front of him, he said, "Worthy musicians! If you will proceed to the kitchen, you shall be fed. Once you are there, I shall inform you of Master Talbot's wishes regarding your several performances during the next few days."

He repeated himself in French.

The kitchen was hot and smoky with the clattering commotion of food preparation. As many as five cooks and their assistants were at work. As for the musicians, seventeen of us—plus one reciter of tales—sat around a long trestle table. For the most part, people separated themselves into groups according to language.

Seated among the English musicians, I heard much talk about travels, where each had played, as well as the news from London. There was gossip, too, about Richard, the new boy king of England, and his court.

"It's said," asserted one of the musicians, "that he loves food, books, and fine fashion. Quite French. As for his taste in music, I fear I have no knowledge yet."

Elena and Woodeth were quite chatty, but Rauf and Gerard said little. As for the food we ate, it was wonderful fare, better than I had ever eaten: barley bread, bacon, onion, garlic, leeks, even something called a jannock: an oat bread. Watered wine and ale were also offered. My hunger was well appeased.

As we concluded our feast, the steward reappeared and, reading from a long scroll, delivered his orders, telling each group in what sequence they would ascend to the balcony during the feast days. There would be many performances.

Our group retreated to the alleyway before our sleeping stall. There Elena led us in practice sessions of the songs and melodies she wished us to play.

All this took us into the early evening. Betimes, I became

more than ready to sleep. I asked for and received permission to go into the stall. Owen came with me. But as before, Woodeth was sent to stand sentry over us. When we entered the stall, she placed herself as great a distance from us as possible. "Do not give me any trouble," she scolded.

Owen and I settled into a far corner, burying ourselves in straw. Once there, and with Woodeth keeping her distance, I was finally able to tell Owen of my encounter with the boy who was selling the Icelandic fish.

"Do you think you can find the Icelanders?" he asked.

"I'll go to the market in the early morning," I told him cautiously. "God willing, I'll find them."

Owen was silent for a while. Then he said, "Will you tell them about me?"

"Of course."

He moved closer. "Crispin," he warned, "they're keeping close watch on us. They won't be happy to find you gone."

He was right, of course. "I have a few coins," I said after some thought. "I'll find something to purchase to soothe their tempers. Now best get to sleep."

Owen settled down. Taking my own advice, but with my mind set on the morrow and what it might bring, I too closed my eyes. Sleep came quickly. But I was not to slumber for long. Perhaps it was because I fell asleep so early. Maybe I was already thinking of rising in the morning. But—at some time—as I lay half buried in the straw, Rauf's voice woke me.

"It was as I thought," I heard him say, though he was trying to keep his voice low. It was, however, slurred with drink, and just loud enough for me to hear.

"The soldiers were an easy purchase," he continued rather brashly. "God's blood, the captain to whom I spoke earns but eight shillings a day. The devil take them all! I promised him five pounds' value if he'd let us through the gates without a search. He could hardly contain his glee. And when I told him I'd offer up a thief to satisfy the magistrates, he was even more willing."

"To everything?" It was Elena's voice.

"Everything!"

"Shh! And you trust them?"

Rauf laughed. "Money binds trust. Have no fear; I'll work my way with some of the other soldiers with as much ease." He laughed. "God's blood—*they* earn but eight pence a day."

"Fine," said Elena. "I'll seek a trader and bargain a passage.

"Now, then," she went on, "the wedding will take place

in two days. Starting tomorrow night, these people will spend most of the time at tables. But they must sleep sometimes." Her voice became lower. "Right after we play will be the best time for you to go about the house and—" She cut herself short.

"Don't worry," Rauf scoffed. "I've already sifted about. It's a rich house."

"The morning following the wedding," Elena went on, "there will be more festivities. That will be the best time for us to slip away."

"Agreed."

"Now get some sleep," Elena urged. "We'll need our full wits on the morrow. I don't wish to stumble and lose all."

"Amen to that."

There the talk ended, though I heard Elena murmur a prayer. Then they too burrowed into the straw and soon were asleep.

I lay there pondering what I had heard. That they were planning to plunder the house was not news. It was the thief Rauf intended to use to satisfy the magistrates that worried me. I didn't think it would be his brother or his wife. In truth, I could think of no one else that he might mean but me.

Though hardly a surprise, the notion was enough to bring a tightness of breath, as if my throat was being clutched. It was not difficult to grasp what it meant: Owen and I had but one day to make good our escape.

23

DID NOT SLEEP much that night. I am sure I heard the bells for lauds. From then on, sometimes dozing, sometimes not, I lay still until the call for prime rang clear.

I sat up. It being cold and damp, I was grateful for my new clothes. In the alley across the way, upon the wall, an all-but-gutted candle burned in a hanging lantern. By its shadowy light, I counted the whole family—including Schim, who was tucked close to Owen. With great care— for I had no desire to wake anyone—I came to my feet and slipped out of the stall.

Once free, I made me way along the alley until I came to the stone-paved street. Shafts of light from surrounding houses enabled me to see. I heard few sounds.

I headed for what I believed would be the city's center, the marketplace. By the time I reached it, though the sky was only a faint gray-blue, the market was already busy with soldiers on patrol. Torches on poles shed enough light to reveal open stalls and pavilions. Here and there a brazier hot with glowing charcoal drew men to warm their hands and turn their faces red. Many more men, their breath misting the chilly air, were pushing barrows and carts, hauling canvas bales of wool. Others were shifting large bundles, sometimes partly opening them, so the fleece could best be seen. The market air smelled of raw and greasy wool.

I made my way through the wool section—the largest part of the market—around the central watchtower. My nose led me to the fish market. Here, too, business was brisk. Boxes, baskets, and tubs of fish, fresh and dried, were everywhere. So too were oysters and cockles. Throngs of people were selling as well as making purchases.

I wandered about looking for I knew not what. I did spy a burly man with a leather apron standing behind what looked to be a barrel of black eels, the eels twisting themselves into knots.

"Please, sir," I asked, "do you know where I might find Iceland fish?"

He looked at me with disdain. "I don't know what you're talking about," he said with a scowl.

"Iceland fish."

"Fish is fish. These are eels." He dismissed me with a wave of his hand.

I went on. I had to inquire twice more before I heard: "Stockfish from Iceland!"

I hastened forward and found a woman standing before some piled wicker baskets full of dried fish. Though her face was weathered, she was young, indeed comely, with round, sun-dark cheeks and bright blue eyes. Her fair, braided hair was wrapped around her head like a crown. The wool jacket she wore was colored blue.

As I approached, she smiled, held up a gray fish by its stiff tail, and fairly brayed, "Stockfish from Iceland!"

Behind her were two men, one old and white bearded, the other young and stubble chinned. They were stacking empty baskets and loading them into a two-wheeled cart.

I stood before the young woman, staring up at her, trying to find words to speak but afraid to. What if she turned me away?

"Do I look so odd to you that you must stare, boy?" she asked as if amused. Her speech was different to my ear: somewhat harsh, with a rough catch that seemed to come from her throat.

"No, mistress," I managed with a bob of my head.

"Then do you want to purchase some fish?" she asked,

not unkindly. "Or have you never seen an Icelandic stock-fish before?"

"Your . . . fish," I stammered. "Are . . . are they truly from that place called Iceland?"

"God's truth and glory," she said, her eyes laughing. "That they are. Which makes them the best. The King of Norway starts his day with them each morning."

I forced myself to look up. "And you, mistress, are . . . are you from that Iceland?"

She looked at me quizzically. "No more. We live in Bergen now. Norway."

"Is . . . Iceland close to Calais?"

Her cheerful face bloomed into a smile. "It's above and beyond the northern seas, and then twice as far as that. More than a thousand miles from here. Why so full of questions?"

Though shocked to learn that Iceland was that far, I took a deep breath and said, "Please, mistress, I . . . I wish to go there."

The young woman stared at me as if I had said the most remarkable thing. She even turned and called to one of the men—the old one—in a different tongue. He halted in his work, peered around, and then stomped forward and considered me gravely.

The man's face was fringed with a thick, snow-white

beard, a contrast to his deeply dark-tanned face, which bore many lines spreading from his deep gray eyes. Yellow-white hair reached his shoulders. He wore a coarse brown belted gown that reached his raw knees. Around his scraggly neck was a cord attached to a sheathed dagger that hung beneath his arm. Seeing a resemblance to the young woman, I took them to be father and daughter.

"To Iceland, boy?" he bellowed. "You say you wish to *go* to Iceland?"

The force of his voice made me step back. "Yes, sir. I . . . do," I struggled to get out.

He considered me, then turned toward the young man who had been laboring with baskets. "Mord!" he called, and spoke something to him in his language.

The young man—grinning—put aside his work to join the others. Short, with brawny arms, the fellow had enough resemblance to the old man to suggest close kin, too. What they also shared was the reek of fish.

The old man stared down at me, his face showing amusement one moment, exasperation the next. "Now then, boy," he said, "it's the rare soul who wishes to go to Iceland. By Saint Thorlac of blessed name, it's mostly the opposite. Why, no sooner did I arrive at this appalling place than I lost my two mariners. Ran off! May the devil swallow them by their tails! God's truth! Now, who are *you* and why should a boy want to go there? The Englishman who goes there is as rare as a mermaid."

Having no idea what mermaids were, I said, "Please, master, my name is Crispin. It's just . . ." There I faltered, fearful of explaining too much. "I just wish to go," I said.

"He just wishes to," the man said to the others mockingly. "And what would you do if you got there?"

"Live," I blurted out, which truly was all I wished.

"Live!" he echoed, with much laughter, showing good white teeth. "If you wish to live there, you must be fleeing some brute of a master."

I tried to stand tall. "I'm a freeman, master."

"But by My Lady, not such a large one. Nor very strong, either, I'll wager."

"I can work hard," I protested. "And . . . and I can bring another with me."

"As big as you?" asked his daughter, smiling.

I nodded earnestly.

"My name is Thorvard," said the old man. "Thorvard Hjalmarsson. My son, Mord Thorvardsson. My daughter, Halla Thorvardsdotter. Once from Iceland." He spat upon the ground as though disgusted. "Now from Bergen in Norway. We speak English because we trade with

Englishmen." He held out his large hand.

I took it. It was calloused, his fingernails yellowing and cracked. The other two crowded close, full of grinning cheer, poking each other as if telling jests.

"Mind, once to Iceland," Thorvard went on, "there's little beyond!"

I could only nod.

"What might you know of ships and sailing?" demanded Thorvard. "We sail an old cog."

"I've sailed one."

"Not in northern seas, I'll wager," said Mord. "Not in winter."

"In storms," I assured him, which was true.

"Even so," said Thorvard, "it's a long way to Iceland. Not many voyage there at this time of the year." He plumped a heavy finger on my chest. "It's brutal work to sail northern seas."

I forced myself to stand still as if to demonstrate my bravery. "I'm . . . not afraid."

He glared down at me. "If we are to get there before full winter is upon us, we must leave—God and wind willing— soon. Say, tomorrow at dawn. But as I said, we're short of men. I'll offer this much: come back at the end of day. If I can't find anyone, better a minnow to chew than no fish at all. Did you say there were two of you?"

"Yes, master."

"Good! Come back, and I'll see what has transpired. I may have no choice but to take you on."

Grateful for even that, I bobbed my head and turned to go when he called. "Boy! What do you know about Iceland?"

I swung back. "If it pleases, master," I said with knowing, "Iceland is a land without kings, or lords, or armies. Men live in freedom there."

"Freedom?" He laughed loudly. "Who told you that?"

"A . . . good man."

"Good? If the one who told you such things believed them, he was the devil's own fool. Maybe such was true one or two hundred years ago. Not now. Iceland is ruled by Norway's king. Bad rule, but rule it is. Håkon the Sixth he's called. As for lords? We have them. Armies? Men can and will defend their families and kin. Often. And they don't do so alone. Soldiers? You may be sure they're there.

"Yes, some live in peace, but many don't. We have our earls, our bishops. The land itself is full of anger. Cold and hot burst forth all the time. In short, Iceland is as far from Eden as it is from here!"

I was so stunned by his words, all I could do was stare

at the man, searching for some hint that he was teasing. "Is . . . that . . . true, what you just said?" I got out, hardly able to breathe.

"As God is my witness!" he roared. "Iceland's an awful, godforsaken place! Here! Ask my children."

Halla, the young woman, perhaps sensing I was upset, nodded solemnly but said, "It's a beautiful place!"

My very soul was shaking. I could barely stand. Somehow I managed to murmur, "I'll . . . I'll come back, master. I . . . promise."

Reeling, I turned away only to see Elena on the other side of the market.

24

 URE THAT ELENA was searching for me, I hastily ducked away and, keeping low, scurried around the fishmongers. Only when I thought it safe did I try to see where she had gone. Since she was short, moving quickly, and the day not yet very bright, it took a while to locate her.

As I watched, I saw her go from stall to stall, talking to the sellers much as I had done. I glanced toward my Iceland man, fearful she would go to him. By God's grace, she did not. Then I realized she was only doing what she'd told Rauf she'd do: seek a voyage to England. But I had to believe she was also looking for me.

Half running, I circled around, wanting to find some place to gather my tumbling thoughts. I moved from the market and made for the outer rim of the city, near the walls. All the while I tried to keep alert, ready to bolt in case anyone from the family came into view. It was by keeping such a constant watch that this time I saw Rauf.

There were moments I truly thought these people were devils bent on tormenting me!

Rauf was standing with a group of soldiers before the open door of a tavern built against the city walls. The sign over the tavern door portrayed a golden lamb. Among the soldiers was the very captain I had seen at the city gates. The same one who had questioned me.

At first the soldiers and Rauf seemed to be doing no more than talking. But as I watched, I observed Rauf drop coins into each of their hands. I had little doubt: he was selling me.

I backed away in haste, and then dashed down one of the side streets, intent on a quick return to the stables. I braced myself for a scolding, or worse.

But as I ran along, I came upon a church so small it might have been a chapel. Desperately wanting some time to calm my spinning thoughts, I darted inside.

It was dark and cold within, the air touched by a trace of incense. A small and solitary candle burned on the altar. Its light illuminated the cross, which bore the broken figure of Jesus. The floor was stone, covered with old, dry rushes that crinkled beneath my step. Walls were stone, too, with paintings too faded for me to see what tale they told.

I looked for some sign, some picture as to which saint was sacred there to make acknowledgment. It was too dim. And I was too upset to make a study. But I did see that against one wall was a tomb, placed so the morning's light fell there first. It rather looked like a table, its top supported by thick pillars. On this slab lay the sculptured form of a rich lady, her long-fingered hands—made of stone— clasped in calm and everlasting prayer.

Would that I was as peaceful! I fell to my knees, bowed my head, and pressed my shaking hands together. As soon as I did, I began to sob, deep body-racking sobs, as if the very calmness I had sought gave vent to my anguish. In my head I kept hearing what Thorvard claimed: that Bear's words about Iceland were false. That nothing good was there. That I would never find my freedom.

But how—I asked myself again and again—could Bear have told me something so wrong? How could he have not known? Did he not know everything?

My heart raged and cried. Even as I wept, a storm of anger at Bear swept through me—a sense of betrayal, a piercing pain that cut my heart and caused me to cover my face with my hands. How could he tell me something untrue! Were all my struggles to go to Iceland for naught! How could I take Owen to such a place? Would I not be free there? Bear had not known! A liar! I hated him! All I could do was weep. I was lost!

The choice that loomed before me—to stay or flee—seemed appalling! To stay meant I would be hanged in exchange for the family's thievery and murder. But if I should flee to Iceland, I would be going to a very distant place that offered nothing of what I wanted! Where I might not be any better off than where I was!

But in the end—in my desperate state—it seemed to me that Iceland—whatever it might be—offered a small grain of hope—which is to say, life—and that little hope was better than what Elena's family had planned for me.

"Dear God," I whispered, "bring me some kind of

miracle, some kindness, that we might go off with that Icelandic ship—if that man will only take us."

But how could we get out of Calais? It was walled. Harder to get out than in, I had been told. I could see that for myself. And soldiers were everywhere. Soldiers, paid to catch me.

"Dear Saint Giles," I whispered to the empty darkness. "I need you so much now. It's all too hard. I'm too young. I can't do this by myself. I beg you! Help me! Tell me what I should do!"

Alas, no voice or vision was bestowed on me.

I remained in the chapel for some more moments, trying to settle myself. How long I remained there, I don't know. I even gazed upon the stone lady, wishing that I were her! Then, quite abruptly, I realized I must get back to the house and the family before Elena and Rauf. To do otherwise would make things even worse.

First, however, I had wits enough to search hastily about in the food market and, for a halfpenny, purchase three apples. They would be, I could only hope, my bribe to the family to excuse my absence.

I raced back to the merchant's house. Once I found it, I plunged around to the back alley and went to the stable stall.

Standing there was Rauf, waiting for me.

"Where were you?" he yelled, his anger as immediate as it was intense.

"At the market," I said. Behind him, Woodeth was watching. So were Gerard and Elena. Owen was in a corner, looking terrified.

"Who gave you permission to go?" Rauf demanded.

"No . . . one." I drew out the apples and presented them as an offering. "I went to get these . . . for all."

He reached out and knocked my hands. The apples flew all which ways.

"Not for one moment are you to go off alone!" he shouted. "Is that understood? You're to stay with us. Always! With me!"

"If it pleases—"

Furious, he swung the full weight of his hand against the side of my head. It was so unexpected, I fell to the ground in pain and dizziness. Before I could recover, he stepped over me and kicked me in my side. "Do you under-stand me now?" he cried.

"Yes . . ." I managed to say, in great pain. I wanted to strike back, but I knew it would be useless.

He bent over and shook his fist in my face. "You're to do only as I say!"

My side throbbing, my nose bleeding, I remained on

the ground, hoping to be left alone. But the next moment he grabbed my arm and hauled me up. "Come with me!"

Too stunned to resist, I allowed myself to be dragged away. None of the family tried to interfere.

Rauf shoved me out of the stall and into the alley.

"Where . . . where are we going?" I said, smearing the blood away from my face.

"The night watch wishes to meet you!" he said, and shoved me forward.

He marched me out to the street, constantly pushing and shoving. Soon enough I realized where we were going: the tavern where I had seen him talking to the soldiers. Was he to hand me over to them right then?

When we reached the tavern, we went inside. It was a large, dark, and smoky room, the ceiling low with heavy beams, with one small, open window and a hearth burning wood. Set about the room were heavy oak tables, with men sitting around them. For the most part, they had tankards before them, while a few had trenchers from which they were eating.

In the far back was a high table. A large man with a stained apron over his bulging belly was using a ladle to pour drinks from a barrel into tankards, which were then served by a woman.

Rauf—still gripping me tightly by my arm—took me into a corner where some soldiers were seated around a table, drinking. Among them I recognized the captain, the same one whom I had seen him talking to a short time ago.

Rauf shoved me forward. "This is the boy I told you about."

The soldiers looked up at me with, at most, indifference.

The captain nodded and said, "You need not worry. We've marked him now."

The other soldiers laughed. One cried, "He'll barely weight the noose."

I recalled the gallows I had seen upon the strand.

Rauf pulled at me anew, this time leading me out of the tavern.

"There," he said, without releasing me, "don't doubt it but they know you now."

Though I was sure I understood what he had done, I asked, "Why did you bring me?"

"So they might know you as one of us," he sneered. "It's the love I have for you, Crispin. When we leave the city, I wouldn't want them to take you up, would I? Now let's go back to the others." He gave me a shove, and I stumbled on.

For my part, I was perfectly aware that he had made it even harder for me—and Owen—to escape.

25

AUF AND I returned to the stall and the family. When we got there, Rauf shoved me away from him.

"Well?" Elena said to him.

"Done," he replied meaningfully, but said no more.

Humiliated, I staggered into a corner. There I fell upon my stomach, face pushed into the straw so no one would see me or my tears. I swore by all the apostles I'd get away from these people or die. Perhaps it would be better to go back to England. Anywhere. My fear was that we had too little time to change plans.

In the end, if I had any doubts that Iceland—no matter what it was—would not serve me better than this, such notions dissolved. For the moment, however, all I could be was patient.

For most of the day, Owen and I were given little choice: we were kept in the stall like prisoners. I so wanted to tell him about my meeting with the Icelanders, and from time to time the boy looked at me with sad eyes full of questions. But I, fearful of being overheard, dared not speak.

At one point Elena, Rauf, and Gerard went off to talk

in private. As before, Woodeth stayed to watch over us. Even so, I didn't dare talk to Owen. I did not trust her. The boy seemed to understand and kept his silence.

When Elena returned, she stood over me, head tilted slightly to one side in that gesture of puzzlement she sometimes had. I rolled away, having no desire to look at her.

"Where did you go this morning?" she asked.

"To the market, where I bought those apples," I muttered.

"Is that all?" she asked suspiciously.

"I stopped in a small church. To pray. I was not gone for so long." What I said was true enough, if hardly complete.

She sighed and said, "Ever the pious one. I'm sorry Rauf acted as he did."

"Why did he beat me?" I asked.

"He has a pointed temper" was all she would say. "It's not always well aimed. I've made him promise he won't do that again."

I did not believe her. But then I too was lying. The thought came: live with liars, become a liar.

"Will you still wish me to play music with you?" I asked.

"Of course," she answered, then turned away. Instructing Woodeth to remain, she went off somewhere.

At length I sat up and looked about. I had no idea where Rauf and Gerard were, though I was just as happy not to be in their company.

Owen and I kept to ourselves at the back of the stall, Schim with us. Woodeth posted herself by the entryway. There was no way the two of us could get by her. Regardless, I did not have the strength to try.

For my part, I kept thinking of how I was going to get back to Thorvard. And if I did, would he be willing to take Owen when he learned how young and small he was? What if he said no to the boy? What should I do? I had to remind myself he had not positively said he would take me. Only if he could not find some mariners.

I don't know what the others did that day. They came and went, though one of them always remained on guard. Even when I went to the cesspit, I was followed.

When Rauf finally reappeared, he glowered at me—as if I were at fault—but thankfully kept his distance. Schim grimaced at him with anger. Twice we were brought food and drink. None of them talked in front of us.

By early afternoon Woodeth was again guarding us. As she sat there, bored, she fell into a doze, breathing the breath of sleep. Only then, in a quick whisper, did I tell Owen about the Icelandic folk. I admit, though, I did not tell what I'd learned about the place.

"Do you think they'll truly take me?" he asked.

I nodded. "But I must get back to them before the day is out."

"How can you?"

"I don't know," I confessed.

"Could I?" he suggested.

"Brave boy. But it has to be me."

The afternoon was waning and I was becoming increasingly uneasy: I *had* to speak to the Icelandic people. Elena was now our guard. I was about to go on my knees and beg her to let me go when one of the steward's servants appeared.

"I'm in need of assistance," he said, addressing Elena. "The benches in the hall must be placed around the tables. The steward said I could have your boy for a time."

Elena looked at me and then at the servant. "Will you be sure to keep a good watch on him?"

"Of course," he returned gruffly, and beckoned me to come.

I looked to Owen and gave a small nod in hopes he would understand I was going to try and reach the Icelanders. Then I hurried out of the stall and followed the servant.

The task required of me was simple enough. Another

boy and I carried some fifteen benches from the main court-yard into the banquet hall. I never knew the other boy's name or he mine. It didn't matter. We did as we were told. The task soon being done, as I had hoped would happen, the steward's servant dismissed me and told me I should return to my masters.

I did not hesitate for a moment. I raced through the courtyard, out the front door, and headed for the market. Determined to avoid anyone from the family, I ran through the streets in an irregular fashion. When I reached the market edge, I paused. It was not as crowded as in the morning. That meant there was greater ease in spying members of the family. But it also meant I, too, might be seen.

Haste, however, was foremost in my mind. Knowing no second opportunity would be had, I ran across the market, making for the spot I had seen the Iceland people.

This time only Halla, the old man's daughter, was there. She was behind the baskets calling "Iceland stockfish!" to the few who passed.

I went and stood before her, fearful of even looking up and too breathless to speak.

"Ah! The boy who wishes to go to beautiful Iceland."

With my chest tight enough to burst, I forced myself to look up and nod. Her pretty face showed amusement.

"Even now, hearing what my father said?" she asked.

"It will . . . it will be enough, mistress."

She grinned. "You must not believe all he said. He's had family feuds over land. He's bitter. The people there are not bad. And the land is beautiful. Full of fire and ice."

I could only nod.

"But he's surely right about one thing," she continued. "It's hard getting there. No easy jaunt. He didn't exaggerate. Have you thought to that? It can—will—be treacherous. God's holy name, it's many a storm that has shaken his old beard! It's not just age that turned it white."

"I'm willing."

"Dark, dreary, and long," she warned, her face now solemn.

The pain in my chest was enormous. I went down on my knees. "Please, I must go."

Halla gazed at me as if I were a puzzle. Her voice softened. "Why so desperate, boy?"

"I . . . I wish to live in freedom," I said.

"Freedom!"

I could only nod.

"Poor creature. Are you threatened here?" she asked. "Trying to escape a beating? A hanging?"

I had become so frantic I could no longer speak. I could

only hope my eyes—welling with tears—spoke for me.

"There's something else here," she said. "You need to speak to me true. I'll not harm you."

"Mistress," I forced myself to say, "if I don't go . . . I'll be murdered."

"Murdered?"

I nodded.

"By whom?"

"Thieves . . . devils."

"Have you done some great wrong?"

I shook my head.

I heard her sigh. "Tell me your name again."

"Crispin."

"Crispin . . . so be it. We've not been able to find any mariners. My father said that if you returned you could come with us—"

My heart leaped. "Blessings on you, mistress. With my friend?"

"He agrees. But pay heed, Crispin. We leave tomorrow at dawn, if tide and wind are willing. Our cog is called the *Stjarna*. That's 'star' in your tongue. My father told me to say you *must* be there. If not, we'll leave without you. Understood?"

All I could do was nod.

Halla smiled. "In Iceland, loyalty is all. And may two boys, with the help of Saint Nicholas, do the work of one man." She held out her small hand as if to make the bargain.

Hardly knowing what to say, I took her hand and kissed it. "We'll . . . we'll be there!" I blurted out, and jumping up, ran as fast as I could back to Master Talbot's house, only hoping I'd not been missed.

26

 S I RACED BACK, I tried to think of the best way I could get in the house without being noticed by the family. It was not a beating I feared but the discovery of my plans to escape.

I went straight for the front door, the main entryway. As before, a servant was standing there. Others were coming and going, loaded with food and whatnot. I ran straight up and said, "One of the musicians," and without waiting for permission, plunged past the door. I was not restrained. Without stopping, I went into the courtyard and then sprinted for the banquet hall, hoping to go back to the stable stall in the same way I had come.

Master Throckmorton was there, surveying the hall. As soon as he saw me, he cried out, "You there, boy! Move these candelabra from here to there."

More than happy to oblige, I did as ordered, saying nothing. When I put the candelabra where he desired, he stepped back, only to tell me to move it somewhere else. This he did any number of times.

In the midst of this task, Elena stepped into the hall. In a glance, she saw the steward and me at work. I paused and looked at her.

"Good master steward," she called. "Do you still have need of the boy?"

"The boy?" said the man, hardly noticing who or what I was. "For a few more moments." He directed me to move the candelabra yet one more time.

Elena waited impatiently.

"There," he said when I'd done as he bid. "That will be enough. Be off with you."

I bobbed my head and went to where Elena waited. She scrutinized me. "You've been away a long while."

"He kept me busy," I replied.

"A self-important man. Now come along."

She led the way back to the stable. The rest of the family was there. Rauf, upon seeing me, looked his angriest. Elena stepped in front of him. "You needn't have worried," she said. "The steward was keeping him at work."

To my relief, Rauf's anger eased, and I received no more than his glowering look.

I went to the back of the stall, where Owen and Schim were waiting. I sat down. The boy gazed at me, eyes beseeching news of what had happened. Not even looking at him, I murmured, "A ship is waiting. We must leave at dawn."

He let go a long breath, as if he'd been holding it the entire while I'd been gone.

Woodeth came and sat near us. She said nothing. But it was perfectly clear we would be guarded as closely as possible so we could not get free. In other words, we were to be held hostage until their thievery was complete.

As I sat there, I considered the three necessary things we must do: flee from these people, get out of the city, and get to the Icelandic boat.

Great Lord Jesus, I thought, let it be!

From that moment on, I remained alert for the smallest chance of escape. Alas, no occasion came that afternoon. We were guarded too tightly.

At one point Rauf offered me those three apples I

had bought and told me to practice my juggling—to keep me busy, I suppose.

Then as night drew on, I realized that the city gates would close at compline. At that point, even if we had gotten away from the family, we would have been unable to leave the city. And then there would be the night watch. Thanks to Rauf, the soldiers would know me on sight.

To make things more difficult, that evening the first of the wedding banquets was to be held. Since all the musicians were to take part in the festivities, we would be included. I supposed Rauf would make sure to put me in the forefront of the family that I might be widely recognized—much the way he had brought me to the soldiers. So it proved.

How I despised Rauf!

When our time to perform came, we advanced to the balcony, which overlooked the hall. We got to it by a narrow, twisting flight of steps, up from the kitchen area.

The kitchen—hot and smoky with its open fires—was in a continual commotion of food preparation, with cooks, servants, servers, helpers, and cleaners in an unending frenzied storm of work. Some cooked. Some colored the food red, blue, or green, even gilding it with gold! Others shaped food into forms, making it look like a swan, a castle, a ship— all to be eaten. One attached peacock feathers to a bird made of sweetmeats! The perspiring, bellowing steward presided over all like a commander at battle with his army.

Every course of food and drink was brought to the table by a parade of servants in multicolored livery and was announced by trumpets blaring gloriously. For each change of dish, a different group of musicians was brought out to play. While we waited, we were occasionally offered food left uneaten by the banquet guests. There was much.

I took silent note that from time to time Rauf wandered off. Where he went, I had no idea. I suspected he was searching about the house. I imagined him taking an inventory of what he intended to steal and entertained hopes he would be caught.

In all this time, Owen and I were never left alone, not for a moment. That meant the boy had yet to hear what I had agreed with Halla. The news fairly burned within me.

When the family's turn to perform finally arrived, we trooped up the steps to the balcony while some Flemish musicians came down. Once on top, we could look and see who and what was there.

Directly across from us, at the other end of the hall, was the bride-to-be, the first I had seen of her. To my great surprise, she was hardly older than eleven or twelve years— younger than Troth. Seated in the center of a raised table, she was dressed like a lady in a fine silk kirtle of green and blue, with long sleeve tippets touched with lace. Her hair was braided in careful circles over her ears, a bejeweled gold band holding all in place. Yet, for all this womanly attire, I was struck by how girlish she was. Moreover, despite all the festivity, she sat stiffly, staring out at those who sat before her with a look of someone dazed.

To either side of the girl sat older women. Perhaps one was her mother; I could not tell. There were also men at that front table—garbed in rich finery—all quite old, with forked beards, and one or two bald heads. I presumed one must be her father—Master Talbot. I did wonder if one of these old men could be her intended husband. I could not tell. None of the men paid attention to the girl, or she to them. I had never given her—the object of all this activity—any thought before. Now I found myself feeling pity for her.

Right below us, at the tables, were many guests, sixty or more in number, men and women. None were of the bride's age.

The display of clothing and color was dazzling: hats, gowns, capes, sleeves, tippets, furs and feathers, elegant boots, gloves, tunics, long sleeves of more color than I could name. Everything seemed encrusted with gold, feathers, silver, and jewels. Here and there, like sprinkled salt and pepper, were the white and black cassocks of priests. Everyone was talking, a constant bubbling babble.

As soon as the trumpets had sounded, Elena called upon us to play, and so we did. For the most part, we performed cheerful tunes—the harp, drums, mandola, recorder, and bagpipe—playing well together.

As I had guessed he might, Rauf ordered Owen and me to go forward. "Owen! Take Schim!" he commanded. "Make him do his tricks. Crispin, juggle! Amuse the bride." It was, I was sure, another effort to display me to as many as possible.

We went to the front of the balcony. Owen set the monkey on the rail. He got the beast to somersault on command. Then Owen began to beat his drum. I commenced to juggle.

The bride looked up, her face transformed from dull indifference to one of glee. She clapped her hands and turned to one of the women seated next to her and pointed up to the balcony—to Schim, I believed.

When Schim—on Owen's command—jumped up and down, all the while grinning, the girl bride laughed and applauded yet again. A number of the guests turned and looked at us, pointing, gesturing.

I turned toward Rauf. He nodded his approval. He had gotten us the attention he desired.

Shortly after, a new course was announced, and we were ordered to descend from the balcony. A group of other English musicians replaced us and, following the trumpet flourish, began to play.

Meanwhile, in the kitchen, we were given food and drink and then directed back to our stall. The talk was less about our performance than about the wealth of the guests. The family's anticipation was blatant as they imagined what lay in store for them. And though they kept Owen and me close, for the most part they paid us little mind.

Unexpectedly, the harried steward appeared and cried, "Young Mistress Talbot, the bride, wishes the boys—and especially the monkey—to be presented to her."

Automatically I looked to Rauf. "Of course," he said, and rose as if to come with us.

"Only the boys," said the steward with a dismissive gesture. "And the beast. Just make sure he's tethered."

Once again I looked toward Rauf. He in turn looked to Elena.

"You must bring them back quickly," Elena told the steward. "We need them to perform."

"Of course," the steward replied, eager to leave.

Elena turned to us. "Go," she said.

Owen and I jumped up—Schim on Owen's shoulder—and followed the rapidly walking steward back toward the house, hardly knowing what to expect.

27

ITH THE STEWARD some steps ahead, Owen and I were at last alone. "We need to escape tonight," I whispered hastily. "The Icelandic ship leaves at dawn."

He halted. "But . . . but how can we get away?"

"I'm not sure. Owen," I blurted out, "I'm not exactly sure what we'll find there."

He looked up at me with worried eyes. "But we'll get away from them, won't we?"

I nodded, wishing that I could, at least, be sure of that.

"That's all I care about."

I said no more.

We were led, not back to the banquet, but to a small adjacent room. Lit by smoky candlelight, it was unadorned save for some faded tapestries on the wall. The bride-to-be was sitting upon a red cushion in a large, high-backed chair. The chair made her appear even smaller, younger. Her feet did not even touch the ground, but swung with child-like impatience. The two women with whom she had been seated in the hall stood on either side, like guards.

The steward fairly pushed us through the doorway of the room, made a brief bow, muttered something about pressing duties, and hurried off.

When we first stepped into the room, the girl had been slumped in her chair. As soon as she saw us, she sat up and smiled broadly, bringing her hands together in a clap of excitement.

One of the women by her side gestured to us. "You may come forward," she said.

We drew closer, pausing when it seemed near enough. Once there we bowed.

"Is that a monkey?" cried the girl, bypassing all polite talk. Her voice was as childlike as her appearance.

"It is, mistress," I replied.

"I've heard of them," said the girl, "but never saw one. You, boy," she called to Owen. "Bring him near."

A timid Owen advanced a few steps.

The bride could not take her eyes off Schim. "Is he . . .

is he dangerous?"

Owen shook his head no.

"Is the monkey yours?"

Owen, too awed to speak, only nodded.

"May I hold him?"

One of the women by her side put out a cautionary hand. "Mistress . . ."

"Don't tell me what to do!" cried the girl with sudden anger, slapping the hand away. "I'll be leaving soon enough, and I'll never see you again. For that, at least, I'll be grateful."

The woman's face reddened, but she stepped back.

To Owen, in much a softer voice, she said, "Come, boy, you need not fear me. I'm merely sulky. Bring him to me so I may be cheered." She held out two pudgy, pink hands.

Owen stepped forward, took Schim from his shoulder and, still holding to his tether, offered him to the girl. The girl set the creature in her lap. Schim, as was his custom, sat on his legs and gazed up at her with great curiosity, then reached out and touched her lips and nose. The girl laughed gleefully. "Does he have a name?"

"Schim," I said.

"Must you keep Schim tethered?" she asked, cautiously touching the monkey's fur, stroking it gently.

"I don't think he likes it," I said. "But he might run away."

"By Saint Anne," said the girl with sudden earnestness while gazing into the monkey's face, "I understand the poor creature's fate." She looked from one of the women to the other and said to us, "I'm tethered, too. And for the same reason. I would also run away."

Not fully understanding, I said, "We congratulate you on your marriage, mistress."

"You need not bother," said the girl, her lips pouting. "I don't want to be married! But it will happen tomorrow," she added when one of the women made a movement to protest. "At the Church of Saint Nicholas. Did you know that my soon-to-be husband is older than my father?" She made a sour face, then leaned forward as if to share a secret with Schim. "I don't like to even say his name. But then I can't speak his Flemish language. He smells vile." She sighed. "But my father wills it so," she said to me. "My husband-to-be is a rich trader. That's what matters. Yes, we will marry in the morning. After much feasting and music making—perhaps some dancing—I shall go off to Bruges. By My Lady's grace, I may never be in Calais again. This monkey, even with his tether, is freer than I am. And you"—she meant Owen and me—"are freer yet."

One of the women leaned in. "My lady, you must not—"

"I want you to go away!" the girl burst out. "I beg you! Can't I have one last measure of liberty?"

The two women exchanged looks of alarm.

"If there be any kindness," the girl cried, "I should like a moment with my new friends!"

Flustered, the two moved a step away. "We will be by the door, my lady," one of them whispered.

"Farther!" shouted the girl. Then to us, in a softer voice, "Come closer, so we may talk in private."

I advanced to where Owen was standing, right in front of the girl.

The girl studied Schim with a look of sadness, petting him gently on his head. "If I could exchange places with you," she said to the beast, "I would. Or," she said, nodding now at us, "with you." Her voice became a whisper. "I suppose it's sinful of me," she confided, "but I truly can't win."

Owen stared at her.

"Forgive me," I said. "Can you not object?"

The girl sat back in her chair and glanced, with a frown, toward the doorway, where we could see her women hovering. Leaning forward, she whispered, "No one listens to me."

She studied us intently. "I should like to be free the way you are."

"Mistress," I said boldly, "we aren't free."

"How can that be?"

"Our family is not our true family. They . . . they are holding us."

The girl's eyes grew wide. "Holding . . . you. Truly? Like . . . this monkey?"

I nodded.

"But surely you can come and go."

We said nothing.

The girl slumped back in her chair. Still holding on to Schim, she stared at us for a long time. We stood there, unsure what to do or say. "The world isn't kind," she said, her voice full of sorrow.

For a moment I thought of Troth.

The girl became silent, staring off I knew not where. "What will you take for this monkey?" she suddenly asked. "I'll have him with me. Name any price."

"I . . . don't want to sell him, my lady," Owen said.

"I'll give you whatever you want."

"He's . . . he's all I have," Owen whispered.

"Oh." She sat back, sighing. "Then he, at least, is well loved."

One of her women stepped back into the room. "My lady, your father wishes you to return now."

The girl put her arms about Schim and hugged him gently. The beast examined the braids around her ears.

"My lady . . ." persisted the woman.

The girl leaned toward us. "By Holy Mary, I should like you, at least, to be free. Listen: I have heard my father speak of a tavern. It's called—I think—the Lamb. It's built against the city wall. He said there's a passage there. . . . It's used by smugglers."

She grinned. "Because I'm a girl, they don't credit me with ears. But if you can find that tavern, you might escape the city." Her eyes glittered. "If only you could take me!" she said.

The second woman came into the room. "My lady!" she called more forcibly.

The girl held out Schim to Owen. As he took the monkey, the girl whispered into Schim's ear, "May God grant you your freedom, too."

That said, the girl slid forward in the chair until, stretching, her gown bunched up, her feet touched the floor. She stood and slowly went to the women who were waiting for her by the door. Just as she left the room, the girl looked back at us over her shoulder. Her eyes were full of tears.

We never learned her name.

Owen and I were left alone. I spun about to Owen. "We may be able to get away now." But no sooner did we step away from the room than we found Elena just beyond the door, waiting for us.

"What did the bride want?" she demanded.

"To see Schim," I said.

She only frowned.

We headed back in silence to the stable, where the rest of the family was waiting for us. All I could think about was the secret tavern passage out of the city. It would be the way to go—if I could find it.

"What happened?" asked Rauf as soon as we returned.

"She was just taken with the monkey," Elena said.

"She wished to buy him," I added, instantly regretting saying so.

"Mangy creature!" said Rauf. "I'd be willing." He reached out and gave Schim a pinch, which made the beast screech and cling to Owen in fright. Rauf only grinned and said, "We'd get more for the monkey than the boy."

That evening we played our music from the balcony one more time. It was long past vespers when we were done. By then the girl bride was asleep in her chair. Not even Schim's tricks and jumps could stir her. In faith, no one seemed to pay the girl any mind. How different she was from Owen and me. And yet—how much alike. I almost wished she were coming with us.

Afterward we returned to the kitchen, where we were offered more food and drink. There was some idle talk with other musicians, but I was too distracted to give it my attention. At length, to my relief, the whole family returned to the stall.

Once there Elena said, "We've been told that the wedding will take place at terce. The musicians will be part of the morning procession to and from the church."

I wondered if Rauf would be at the celebration or about the house in search of things to steal.

"The bells have already rung midnight," said Elena. "We need to sleep."

They arranged themselves for the night, as if casually, but I took note that they had Owen and me lie down at the inner part of the stall, the rest blocking the way. Rauf took the outermost position. The night before it had been Elena. As I looked about, I sensed their tension and excitement. I wondered if they were about to embark upon their thievery. While I knew how wrong it was, I rejoiced at the thought. It could well mean they would be leaving Owen and me alone. Getting out of the stable would be much easier.

I was quite certain that the tavern the girl had mentioned was the place where Rauf had shown me to the soldiers. So I put my head to trying to recall the route we had taken there. Would I be able to find it in the night? I wondered if it would even be open. Hopefully those soldiers would not be there. Curfew had long passed. But it was there I intended to go.

Owen and I stayed close. Schim, too. Once we lay down, I managed to whisper into his ear, "We must leave at prime." I had no doubt: we would have but one chance to do so. There would be no second.

"The tavern?" he murmured.

I nodded. We dared not speak anymore. Thus began one of the longest nights of my life.

28

T FIRST ALL was calm and peaceful. The church bells rang their calls to prayer. Matins. Lauds. The lantern outside our stall shed its languid light, occasionally stirred by some

random breeze. From within the house came an occasional clank and thump. No doubt, the kitchen people were preparing for the wedding breakfast feast. I heard the night watch passing, giving their cry, "All's well! All's well."

I lay as still as I could, eyes open, listening as the family settled deep into slumbers: Woodeth's sighs and murmurs. Rauf's deep breathing. Gerard's small sounds. My own slight movement, which made the straw crunch.

I tried not to think about what Thorvard said about Iceland. I preferred to believe Halla. More to the point, I reminded myself that Elena's family intended to deliver me to the Calais gallows. I would have this one chance to escape these people and get on that Icelandic ship. Yes, going there would be an uncertain thing. But—I told myself—far better to risk an uncertain life than certain death.

I thought of Troth. I tried to push aside my anger at Bear. To think that he had been wrong made my eyes smart and my heart feel heavy. As if to turn from him, I sought the blessings of Jesus and Saint Giles. They would not abandon me. No more than I would do that to Owen.

I looked to the boy and gave his hand a light touch as reassurance. He returned it to show me he too was awake.

Shifting, I checked to see how the family had arranged themselves and planned a passage through them. That done,

I tried to remain alert. But despite my desperate desire to stay awake, I fell asleep.

I don't know which came first, the church bells announcing prime or Owen's touch. Perhaps one and the same. It didn't matter. In the instant, I was fully awake.

I lifted my head and looked about. There was a faint glow coming from the lantern just beyond the stall. All else was dark. Owen was fully awake, sitting with his back against the wooden wall staring at me. The monkey lay in his lap, asleep.

I pushed myself up on my elbow. The family lay so deep in the straw it was difficult to determine just who was where. Even so, I made myself note them one by one. I counted the two women and Gerard.

Not Rauf.

Startled, I looked again. There could be no doubt. Rauf was not there.

Very slowly I shifted myself about until I could lean over toward Owen and whisper "Rauf" into his ear. He nodded his head as if to say he already knew. His gaze remained on me, waiting for me to tell him what to do.

Though fearful of Rauf's return, I knew that if we didn't leave then, we'd be too late to get to the ship. I indicated that Owen should leave the stall first.

Owen returned a nod of understanding.

As the boy—Schim in his arms—rose slowly, I dared not breathe. I did have a moment's unease when the monkey woke and looked around, small eyes wide with puzzlement, tail twitching. Owen gently touched the back of his head. The creature responded by pressing his wizened face against the boy's neck, but made no further move. Happily, Owen moved with little sound. Once, twice, he paused when Gerard, then Elena shifted in their sleep. Blessedly, neither woke.

It seemed long—but surely no more than moments—before the boy, with Schim now sitting on his shoulder, stood beyond the stall. The tiny flame in the lantern made Owen's shadow loom large. Once out of the stall he looked around the stable and made a gesture for me to come.

Taking a deep breath, my heart beating very fast, I put my hand to the back of the stall and slowly pulled myself to my feet.

Grateful for the little light there was, I worked to avoid the sleepers, frustrated by the small scrunching sounds my feet made in the straw. Once, twice, I had to stop to calm myself. Each time I looked up and saw where Owen was waiting—his look intense, his large, staring eyes drawing me forward. Even the monkey stared at me, the tip of his tail twitching.

Then Woodeth shifted, which brought me to a halt. Next Gerard swung his arm and actually struck my shin. After a momentary and frightful pause—during which he moved no more—I resumed my forward steps until I, too, stood free of the stall.

Once there we paused in the lanternlight for a brief moment, looking up and down. Then we turned in the direction that would lead us to the street.

Even as we did, Rauf stepped around the corner.

29

E CAME FROM the direction of the house, sack in hand. Even in the morning murkiness, I could see the sack was full, so I had little doubt he'd been at his thievery. In his other hand, he clutched his dagger.

For the smallest part of a moment, the three of us stood in the little light, staring at one another as if each could not believe what the other was seeing.

"Where . . . where are you going?" he hissed in a voice thick with rage. "Get back where you belong!" He pointed his blade toward the stall.

"We're . . . we're leaving," I somehow found voice to say.

"The devil you are!" cried Rauf. Face full of fury, he flung the sack aside and advanced upon us, dagger forward. He grabbed Owen's arm and yanked. The boy cried out. No sooner did he do so than Schim, screeching like a demon, leaped at Rauf's face, biting and clawing.

Attacked so unexpectedly, Rauf thrust Owen away. As the boy fell, Rauf slashed the beast with his blade. The monkey, torn and bloody, fell to the ground.

For one gawking, terrifying moment, I just stood there, appalled.

But Owen became engulfed by rage. He leaped up and, screaming "Murderer!", flung himself at his tormentor, beating upon Rauf with his small and frantic fists. The boy's fury took Rauf completely by surprise. Dropping his dagger, he staggered back, slipping on the monkey's blood and dropping down onto his knees. Owen kept hitting him. A floundering Rauf groped frantically for his dagger.

In that moment I leaped forward, snatched Owen's arm, and dragged him away down along the alley. "Murderer!" the boy kept screaming back. "Murderer!"

At the turning, I paused for just an instant to look back. Rauf had found his dagger and pulled himself up even as shouts erupted from the stall: "Thieves! Thieves!"

It was Elena, shrieking.

"Run!" I shouted. Clutching Owen's hand, I plunged toward the street. But once I reached it, I hardly knew which way to go. The boy was now clinging to me, moaning, "He killed Schim!" again and again.

"Thieves! Alarm!" came cries from behind us.

"Just come!" I yelled at Owen. I hardly knew if he held me or I him, but we raced along until we reached the next crossing. There we turned yet again and went on, taking another turn, and yet one more. There, out of breath, my panic great, I had to pause.

I had no notion which direction to go. My knowledge of Calais, such as it was, was rendered all but useless by my terror and the dark. The deserted streets appeared all the same.

Unable to decide which way to go, I took refuge in the shadowy recess of a deep-set door. Overwhelmed by what had happened, I staggered against a wall and pressed my forehead against a stone. Cold and trembling, short of breath, all I could think was, If they catch us, they'll kill us now.

I felt a pull on my arm. Owen was standing there, looking up at me, eyes large with fright, grimy face streaked with tears. No one could have appeared more wretched.

"He'll try to kill me, too!" he cried piteously. "He will."

Then, even as I stood there, trying to think what to do, I heard shouts: "Murderers! Thieves! Alarm!"

My dread redoubled: they were calling the night watch. We had to get out of the city.

I tried to recall where the tavern the girl spoke of might be. "Stay close to me!" I said to Owen. Though uncertain— but knowing we must move—I stepped away from our hiding place and looked up and down the street. Thin light came from the crescent moon and the array of cold stars above. A hint of dawn glimmered.

"Murderers! Thieves!" came the cry again, from yet a different place. I heard running, the sound of several people's steps. "Back!" I cried, and retreated to the doorway.

Next moment a man, broadsword in hand, raced down the street directly in front of us. God and the shadows provided protection. The man passed on. Though I could not see who it was, I had no doubt he was hunting us.

Once the man had passed, I grabbed Owen and crept out from our hiding place. "Come on!" I commanded, and began to run.

I tried to recognize landmarks—a sign, a door as we

went. Anything. I met with little success. On we went, racing down one street and then another, pausing at each corner while trying to see what danger might lurk ahead.

"Are we going to that tavern?" asked Owen.

"Just stay close."

We reached a turn. That time I recognized a narrow door and was fairly certain the tavern was just beyond. I stole a quick glance. Sure enough, it was there. But so too were a goodly number of men—soldiers among them. They were milling about its door. All were armed. It was the night watch.

Recoiling, I snatched Owen's hand again and tugged him down the street in the opposite direction. I pulled so hard he stumbled to his knees and cried out. I yanked him up and raced on. Only when we had gone around a few more turns did I stop. My side pained me. My breath was labored. Owen, his knee bloody from his fall, was also gasping and gulping for air.

Trying to think, I looked about. The street we were on was deserted. A morning breeze made signboards creak. An excited dog began to bark and was answered by another. From somewhere came those cries: "Murder! Alarm! Murder!"

I plunged through a maze of streets, halting frequently

to look all ways. The shouts of "Murder! Murder!" seemed to come from everywhere. I sensed them closing in, but I still didn't know where to go.

Owen slumped against a wall. "I can't ... I can't go anymore," he gasped.

Needing to think, wanting to give the boy—and me—a rest, I hid ourselves behind some barrels. To my dismay, the sky above was lighter. Dawn was close. It would allow me to see better, but we would also be easier to find. And—to add to my desperation—I knew that the Icelandic ship would be leaving soon.

"Can you go on?" I asked the boy.

He shook his head. His chest was heaving. Tears were streaming along his cheeks.

I squatted down and stretched my arms behind me. "Get on my back!" I said. As he pressed himself against me, I clasped my one hand with the other and so was able to hold him up.

With Owen on my back, I staggered down yet another street. There I saw we had reached the town's edge, where the city wall rose above the houses. I hurried down the alley until I reached it.

"Slide off!"

When the boy dropped down, I examined the wall.

Made of stone blocks, it rose up some seventy-five feet. I reached high and sought to find some finger grip, hoping to haul myself up. The stones, however, were too finely set. I couldn't get a hold. Climbing would be impossible.

"Come on!"

We tried the next street, where the wall continued, but I couldn't climb there either. Even so, we went on for two more streets. This time we had come to a place where walls met. Built into the corner was a stout, round tower with an open entryway. Within it, I could make out a narrow, curving flight of stone steps, which led up.

"This way!"

I dashed inside and tried to see—without success—the top of the steps. All I saw was greater light, which made me think the steps reached the open ramparts. That made me remember I'd seen soldiers there when I first came to the city. What if they were there now?

Even before I could think what to do, I heard the sound of footfalls.

"Someone's coming!" Owen gasped.

We darted up the steps, all but falling up, if such a thing is possible. Upon reaching the top of the wall, I glanced around. What I saw was a wide, stone-paved walkway walled on either side. The walls reached the height of my shoulders. The outer walls had irregular gaps, wide enough to allow soldiers to look out and, no doubt, shoot their arrows and bolts. I could see no one about.

I ran to one of the gaps, hauled myself up, and looked down. Morning's dull glimmer allowed me to see water some hundred feet or so below: the city's double moats.

I jumped back down to the rampart and went to the city-side wall and peered down. I could see streets and low rooftops, as well as churches and watchtowers. At first it seemed deserted; but even as I looked, Elena and Rauf rushed into the street below, the very place where we had been. Both were armed.

They were conferring right below me, turning now this way, now that, as if considering the ways we might have gone. They didn't think to look up, not at first.

Soon as I saw them, I leaped back.

"Rauf and Elena!" I hissed.

"Where?"

"Below!"

I stole another quick glance down. That time I saw Elena pointing up, before turning and running toward the tower steps.

"This way!" I cried, grabbing hold of Owen's hand and racing along the rampart. As we ran, I spied another wall tower ahead of me. This one was not placed at a corner, but midway along the wall. Thinking we could use it to get back down to the streets, I aimed for it.

As I ran, I glanced back. Elena and Rauf had burst onto the wall. It took but a moment for them to see me.

"Crispin! Owen! Stop!"

I redoubled my pace, only to see, from the very tower toward which we were heading, a troop of soldiers bursting forth. A few held torches. Some were armed with swords or crossbows. Leading them was the captain whom Rauf had made me meet.

Upon seeing me, the soldiers stopped.

We were caught between the two: Elena and Rauf on one side, the soldiers on the other.

I swung about, grabbed at Owen, and dashed to the outer wall. I scrambled atop and braced myself between one of the gaps. Owen held up his arms. I hauled him up. I looked back only to see one of the soldiers kneeling, a crossbow pressed against his shoulder. He was aiming it at us.

"Jump!" I cried, and fairly pushed Owen off the wall. Next moment I followed.

 T TOOK BUT an instant before I struck cold water. Down I sank, swallowed by the moat's filth. Gagging and gasping, trying to keep my mouth tightly clenched, I plunged down deep, sinking to such a depth that my foot struck the muck-clogged bottom. Without thinking, I kicked, which reversed my direction and shot me up.

Desperate to reach air, I thrashed my arms and kicked my legs until I burst upon the water's surface. Once there I flailed, spinning and turning, looking desperately for Owen, until my hand struck something soft and slippery. I tried to grip whatever it was, only to slide away. First with one hand and then another, still coughing and spitting, I found a grip and kept myself from sinking a second time. Even so, it took a moment before I realized I was clinging to the city wall.

Shouts came from above. Twisting, I saw torches and faces illuminated by the flames. Like gargoyles, soldiers were peering down through the morning murkiness. But kind fortune had set me on the very inside of the moat, which made it hard for them to locate me.

I pushed myself as flat as possible, trying to decide what to do next, still wondering where Owen was, even as I was in danger of slipping.

My hold gave way. I went down a second time. As I dropped, I swung my body about and kicked back as hard as I could against the wall. In so doing, I thrust myself a good way toward the moat's other side.

The strength of that wild shove carried me halfway across the moat, after which I began a wild flailing and kicking, much as I had done in that ditch to escape the Frenchman. It brought me into the sight and sound of those above.

"There!" came a cry. Arrows hissed by me, once, twice. Striking out in mindless frenzy, I went forward, enough so that I reached the far side of the moat. There I grasped whatever weeds or stones I could, anything to hold me and keep me from dropping back. In such a fashion, I managed to crawl out of the water.

Free of the first moat, I scampered madly from the water's edge and flung myself down on the far side of the mound between the moats. For a few moments I could do no more than lay where I was, dripping wet, shivering, struggling for breath, spewing foul water. I realized I had lost my boots.

Twisting around, I got a glimpse of the wall I had just

left. I saw figures peering down from the walls, holding up torches, looking for me. Having yet to discover where I was, I was safe from their arrows, for the moment.

I still saw no trace of Owen. Fearful he might have drowned, I took the chance to lift my head higher and look about. I caught sight of him: his head was resting on the mound, but from the waist down he was still in the water. I was not even sure if he was alive.

Impulsively, I jumped up and ran toward him.

"There! He's there!" came shouts from the wall.

A crossbow bolt, hissing with invisible speed, shot past, piercing the earth. Its featherwork quivered by my foot.

I reached where Owen lay, gripped his arms with my two hands, and struggled to drag him up the mound. A second bolt went into the dirt.

When I reached the top, I rolled Owen over the crest and then dove after him, even as an arrow struck the ground close to where I stood.

I tumbled down, rolling toward the second moat until I burrowed my fingers into the earth to keep myself from falling back into the water.

Below the mound's crest, above the second moat, I could no longer see the city walls, which meant my pursuers could not see me.

I crawled to where Owen lay on his back. When I turned him over, he began to spit out water, coughing and gagging.

"Owen," I said into his ear. "Owen!"

He shook his head but did not get up.

Relieved that he was yet alive and deciding to let him rest, I pushed myself onto my knees and searched in all directions. In the steadily increasing light, I could see no one. But I knew it would not remain that way for long. They would be coming after us.

I knelt by Owen's side. "Owen!" I called. "We have to move. Quickly!"

Shaking his head like a wet dog, he pushed himself up onto his hands and knees.

"We have to get across the second moat."

"I . . . can't."

"You have to," I told him. "Run down and leap as far as you can. You must do it now! They'll be after us."

For a moment he did nothing. Then, as if by force of will, he abruptly jumped up, raced down the mound, and leaped, with arms churning like windmills, as far as he could. I did just the same, beating my arms as if hoping to take flight.

I hit the water. This time, even as I struck, I swung my arms and kicked. Though I sank some and struggled for breath, I was so determined to reach the far side that I fairly clawed my way across. Once I had, I scratched my way onto land.

Owen had managed to get across too and now lay upon his back, one arm flung over his face. "Good boy!" I called to him.

I sat up and was able to see the road that led to the city and the strand. Despite the early hour, people were already there. That was where we needed to go.

"Owen. We must get to the ship!" I called.

He staggered up. I took his hand and we rushed on. As we went, I wondered what the family and the night watch were doing. Would they think we had drowned? Would they look for us at the strand among the boats? Or would they be at the city gates? How would I find Thorvard? I had no answers.

Owen said nothing but went on doggedly, as much staggering as running. Once he stopped and bent over, retching, struggling for strength.

"Crispin . . ."

I told him to climb on my back again, which he did. Then I ran as best I could, not as *if* our lives depended on it, but because I knew they did.

31

E REACHED the road. Once there we were among many people, all presumably heading for Calais. For the most part, they were peasants and merchants with goods to sell. While I'm sure they considered us odd in our wet and dripping clothing, they asked no questions.

We stayed among them—Owen now on his own legs—going as fast as our strength allowed, all the while keeping alert for signs of our pursuers. As it happened, I noticed five soldiers running along the mound that divided the two moats. They were—praise God!—going in the opposite direction. But I knew that would not be the end of it.

We ran on.

As the road bent around the eastern end of the city, the bay lay before me. Beyond was the gray-blue sea. Two small boats—fishing ketches, with their triangular sails puffed by winds—were gliding out of the bay, passing the island fortress. How I wished we were on one of them!

While the people on the road made for the city gates, we turned toward the sea.

The strand was in plain view. Dozens of boats were

pulled up to the shore or tied to the two wharves. They were crowded with bales and barrels as well as the mariners and laborers working with them.

High above the strand, away from most of the work, we stopped running and scanned the wharves.

"Where is our boat?" Owen asked. He was gripping my hand as if it were the only thing that kept him standing.

Thorvard had told me his ship was a cog, the same kind on which I had sailed from England. I could see three such ships. Two were tied to one wharf, one to the other. I could only pray that one of these was the Icelandic boat. It *was* past dawn, the time the Icelanders had said they meant to sail.

"Look there!" cried Owen, pointing.

I saw them: Gerard and Woodeth hurrying about on one of the wharves, where two of the cogs were tied. They stopped and talked to now one man and then another. While Elena and Rauf had searched within the city, these two must have come directly to the docks.

We darted behind a pile of wool bales, then peeked out and watched. I wondered if they remembered that I had wished to go to Iceland. Was that what Gerard was asking?

I turned back to the single cog and spied a man coming onto the high castle. My heart leaped: he had long white hair and a white beard. Thorvard! He was gazing toward the land, as if in search of someone—hopefully me.

I turned back to watch Gerard and Woodeth. Woodeth was no longer there.

Where could she have gone? Gerard had moved farther along the other wharf. Upon reaching the end, he stopped and appeared to be talking to a laborer. After a few moments, that man shifted and pointed across the way, at the second wharf. I gasped. I was sure he was pointing out the Icelandic ship.

"Hurry!" I cried.

Dragging Owen along, I began to run, darting in and around the many workers and bales of goods. Then there was nothing but a few bales between us and the wharf.

We dashed forward only to have Woodeth step out from behind a bale and stand before us.

We halted. Owen pressed close to me. I could do no more than just look at her.

Woodeth stared back. But then, without a word, she turned away. Though I knew she had seen us, she acted as if she had not. Instead, she hurried toward the other wharf and, by so doing, allowed us to pass by. In haste I murmured a quick blessing on her and then turned to Owen.

"Come on!" I said. When we reached the wharf, we raced along until it reached the cog. A ramp of wooden planks had been set from the wharf to the ship. I paused and looked back. Woodeth was with Gerard again. She was shaking her head as they stepped out on the wharf.

We ran up the planks and jumped onto the ship. Mord was not there. But to my great relief, I saw Halla.

"Ah!" she cried when she saw me, offering up a bright smile. "You've come! Father!" she called back toward the stern. "The boy is here."

The old man on the castle swung around. He gazed down at me, his face fierce. "So you've come," he said, leaning his elbows on the rail, the better to consider us. "Is that the way you work? Ignoring your first order? Didn't I tell you we must leave early?"

"Forgive me, master," I cried. "We came as soon as we could!"

"Did you swim here?" he asked.

"No, master."

"Is *that* your friend?"

I nodded.

Thorvard just stared at Owen.

Desperate, I cried, "Master, have mercy. We're being hunted."

"Ah! There it is! No less than I thought. By whom? Why?"

"I can't explain. Not now," I said, fearful that at any moment Gerard and Elena would appear and haul us away. "I beg you, by all the mercy of Jesus. Let us go with you. It's worth our lives."

"Father," cried Halla, "let them!"

Thorvard made no reply. He looked up at the sky. He looked to his daughter. Then he leaned over the side of the boat and peered back along the wharf. At last he shifted back toward Halla.

"Stow them below," he told her. "And get your brother up here. If we're to leave before the wind eases, we need to hurry."

We raced after Halla. She led us to an open square in the middle of the deck. She called down. "Mord!"

The young man climbed up. She said something in her own language. He nodded.

"Drop down there," Halla said to us, adding in a softer voice, "quickly!"

We sat on the edge of the open space. In the hold below, I saw bolts of cloth and sacks of wheat. I let myself drop down, landing softly on some cloth. Then I turned and caught Owen as he followed. As soon as we were down there, the open area above our heads was covered. The only light was two beams that seeped through chinks in the wood. They cut through the darkness like glowing swords.

Alone, no longer running, utterly spent, my body shuddered with exhaustion, pain, and fear. "Dear Saint Giles," I whispered. "Protect us!" It was the only prayer I could utter. But I kept repeating it.

Owen lay facedown upon the bolts of cloth. I could hear him crying. The best I could do was rest my hand upon his trembling back.

From overhead I heard footfalls on the deck. Then voices. One of the speakers—to my ears—sounded much like Gerard.

After a few moments the voices ceased.

I waited, breathless, afraid to guess what was happening. Abruptly, the silence was broken by a harsh rasping sound. The space overhead was yanked open. The hold where we were hiding was flooded with light. A hand reached down. A voice called, "Crispin! Come out of there!"

Trying to determine whose hand it was, I shrank back. But then all strength seemed to drain from me. I could struggle no more. Though I did not know whose hand it was, I grasped it and was hauled up like some limp sack.

32

ONLY WHEN I reached the deck did I realize it was Mord's hand. His pretty sister was standing by his side, all but laughing at me. Thorvard was there too, looking grim. I glanced about: I saw nothing of Gerard or Woodeth.

I can only guess what I looked like, save that there could have been very little promise: bedraggled, cold, and wet. And very young. Desperation and fright must have been stamped large upon my face.

Perhaps it was my fancy, but I thought I saw a fleeting smile on Thorvard's lips and in his crinkled eyes. He sighed as if, upon full examination, he questioned his judgment in taking us.

"Your self-proclaimed friends," he informed me, "have gone. I'll hear you out later. But if we're to take advantage of the wind, we must make haste. Just know that if your work is worthless, I'll hurl you back into the sea. Let's go!"

I helped Owen out of the hold and told him we were safe. He flung his arms around me in relief.

Mord, meanwhile, went to the bow and began to untie the binding lines. Thorvard went the other way, climbing a short ladder to take his place on the castle by the rudder bar. As for Halla, she brought me to the base of the castle, where there was a windlass, the machine for hoisting the sail. It had a drum that wound a heavy rope, which was connected to the top of the mast and then looped down to the sail yard.

She handed me a wooden handspike and showed me how to insert it into the windlass and turn the wheel. The turning required all the strength I had.

As the large brown canvas sail rose up, it filled with wind, flapping and snapping loudly. Then, with a lurch, the cog heeled, veering from the wharf.

In moments we were moving through Calais bay, passing the island fortress. The city was falling behind us, its walls, towers, and spires becoming smaller.

Mord, having hauled in the wharf ropes, ran back to where we were, shoved me aside, and turned the windlass that much faster, until the sail reached the mast's pinnacle. Then he raced back to lash down the dangling ropes that hung from both bottom corners of the sail. Now taut, the sail filled. Our speed increased.

Thorvard was standing with one hand on the rudder bar, guiding the boat out into the bay. For her part, Halla pounded pieces of wood into the windlass to keep it—and the sail—in place.

Thorvard gave a shout.

Mord turned to me. "He wants you."

Leaving Owen, I climbed the ladder to where Thorvard stood on the castle. His large right hand was on the rudder bar, his eyes fixed somewhere on the water.

"Tell me your name again," said Thorvard.

"Crispin."

"And the other?"

"Owen."

Thorvard shook his head as if in regret. "Crispin," he said, "saints willing, you're going to Iceland, though you look too puny for such a voyage."

"God bless you, master," I replied. "I swear, by the sacred blood of Jesus, I'll work hard for you."

"So you say," he returned with a curt nod. "Pay heed. I speak bluntly. My orders shall be your obligations." He fell into silence.

After a moment I said, "Please, master, how long will the voyage take?"

"No less than twenty days. Perhaps sixty. Maybe forever. We go by the wind, and the wind is God's whip."

Suddenly the cog lifted and dropped, making me stagger while sending a cold spray of water over us. I grabbed hold of a rail. We were now upon the sea.

"There! We're barely out of the bay and you're twice wet," said Thorvard. "Go on now! Mord will set you both to task. Go!" he bellowed when I didn't move. "Your master has given orders. There's needful work!"

I turned away and held on as the ship pitched and rolled among the ocean swells. It was not the movement of the ship that caused me such unsteadiness: it was the pain in my chest.

We sailed all day. For all our exhaustion, we worked throughout, sometimes under the direction of Mord or Halla, sometimes Thorvard.

There was nothing neat or clean about the *Stjarna*. She was a filthy, cluttered boat. Knots of rope lay everywhere midst tools, pieces of wood, parts of canvas bales, even shaggy clumps of wool. In the bow was stored a large stone anchor. The tall mast was set somewhat forward of midship, and from it a tangle of ropes ran down to the deck. I could make no more sense of those strands than if I had been given a book to read.

Night came. On the castle Thorvard steered the ship. Halla had taken to Owen—as he to her—and she was treating him with special kindness. She had even made a bed for him in the hold with bolts of cloth, and he was sleeping the sleep of peace.

I sat near Thorvard by the rail at the high stern.

Waves rolled and sounded. The ship heaved. Our sail snapped and cracked. Now and again the sea sprayed over us. Above us was the vast array of stars. Staring at them, I recalled the night at the convent when I found Troth looking at them. Was she looking at them now? Though she was in her small world and I in this vast one, I hoped we were looking at the same stars.

Thorvard said, "Do you know the stars?"

"Just that they are there."

"Learn the heavens," he said, "and you will know the earth."

"What do you mean?"

He pointed up. "There's a bull. There's a fish. There's Hercules."

"Where?" I said, straining my neck.

Pointing, he began to mark these heavenly bodies by showing me how to draw lines in my head, thereby connecting the stars and turning them into pictures. It was amazing to see it thus. It was as if, by a kind of conjuring, the heavens turned into a vault of images.

Then he said, "And there's Great Bear. There, Little Bear."

My heart jumped, for I had felt much anguish for what I had thought of Bear.

"Bear?" I cried. "Truly? Where!"

He pointed out the picture.

"I had a . . . friend named Bear," I said, my voice thick. "He died not so long ago."

Thorvard considered my words. "To be so well placed in heaven, he must have been a good friend."

"None . . . better."

He studied me. "Is that the one who told you those things about Iceland?"

I nodded.

He grunted. "Then he must have been human—like us."

Quite unexpectedly, I began to weep, hard racking sobs full of the deepest pain.

His voice low and thick, Thorvard said, "For whom are those tears, Crispin? Who are you? Where do you come from? Who was that friend called Bear?"

I said nothing. I could not. It was enough to breathe.

"Well, then," he said, "you need not say. I've seen many a broken boy—was one myself—and you are among the most bent. But perhaps I should ask: why, in Calais, were the people so eager to hang you?"

I did not, could not, and dared not answer right away.

Rather, I was silent a long while, staring up at the stars where he said Bear was. But Thorvard's silence seemed to call on me to speak. Suddenly I felt the need to tell all. Which I did.

While I related everything that had happened to me, I never looked at Thorvard, not once, nor did he say a word. Even when I'd finally done, he remained quiet. Only the sea spoke.

We stood in silence. Then, after a while, he said, "Come here. Stand next to me."

I did so.

He kept one hand on the rudder bar. His other hard hand he set upon my shoulder. Just rested it there, heavy, firm.

"Crispin," he said, "God doesn't make saints for us to think about their perfections. He makes them so the rest of us can consider our sins. Mortals—like you and I—have sinned. Like your Bear."

He pointed up. "Consider that bear. The smaller one. Can you see it clearly?"

"I think so."

"That bright star there—at the end of smaller bear's tail," he said. "Do you see the one I mean? It's called the North Star. Ancient mariners called it Cynosure."

I looked along the reach of his arm and hand and thought I saw what he meant. "What of it?"

"That's the mariner's star. It shows true north. It's always there. Unmoving. Know that star and you shall know where you are and where to go. That star is the sailor's hope and guide. I named this ship after it. Always look for it. It can be your salvation. Crispin, follow your Bear."

My heart seemed to swell. "Will it . . . will it always be there?"

"Until the end of time."

I stared at the star, fixing it in my heart. "Then can I follow Bear forever?"

"Not follow, Crispin. Use. Learn to use him to help you know where you are and where you're going."

My tearful eyes made the star blurry. But I saw it still. And would see it, I knew, till the end of time.

About the Author

AVI is the author of more than sixty books, including CRISPIN: *The Cross of Lead*, a Newbery Medal winner, and CRISPIN: *At the Edge of the World*. His other acclaimed titles include THE TRUE CONFESSIONS OF CHARLOTTE DOYLE and NOTHING BUT THE TRUTH, both Newbery Honor Books, and most recently THE SEER OF SHADOWS. He lives with his family in Colorado. Visit Avi at www.avi-writer.com.